The Night
Of
The Rising Dead

SILVIA CINCA

Brunswick Publishing Company

Copyright © 1985 by Silvia Cinca

Cover by Elena Zlotescu

International Standard Book Number
0-931494-61-3

Library of Congress Catalog Card Number
85-71313

First Original Edition

Published in the United States of America

by

Brunswick Publishing Company
Lawrenceville, Virginia

The Night of the Rising Dead

CONTENTS

THE VOICE

Everything started with a telephone call. He got a wrong number. Could happen to anybody. It was a Sunday evening. These are moments which most people share with someone, or with a bunch of friends. He took the telephone book and started looking for an old acquaintance. How it happened, he could hardly remember. He only knows that he heard a strange voice coming from the other end. A warm voice. Agreeable. First, it merely said: "Wrong number." He apologized and then hung up. Then, he realized he liked that voice. He dialed again. He didn't know what number he had dialed. He tried over and over. On the third try, it was that voice again. He couldn't come up with a lie. He told her he was calling on purpose, to hear her voice. He was expecting to be admonished and told he was bothering her. He made his apology quickly. To his surprise, she answered with the same warmth: "You aren't bothering me at all. Anyway, I was alone." Thus, he found out the most important thing that he could call her again. That he would never annoy her. The woman was wondering what made him call again. "I liked your voice," he said.

"It's funny, I too, liked the sound of your voice," she replied. The next day, he called again. Day after day, they would talk. As soon as he got home from work he would call her. He would tell her that he was back home. And what had happened during the day. So did she. Sundays, they would hang on the phone for hours. Each came to know the other's life. She knew that his wife had left two years before. That he had two kids "of rare beauty," living with him. The boy was in the fourth grade. He had straight A's. The girl was in the second grade, somewhat naughty. The children's mother had remarried. She didn't want to take the children. So, the father was happy to have them both. He loved them very much. In the summertime the children stayed with their grandmother. The father had a three-room apartment in a new building. He told her that he had bought a painting by Van Gogh. He was very proud of his purchase. He loved art. He had an engineering degree. He asked her advice as to where to hang the painting. He asked her advice for whatever he did.

She started coming home from the office earlier than she used to. She would shove all the papers into the drawer at two to three and run home. The people she worked with noticed a change in her. However, they wouldn't ask questions. "She might be in love" — they were thinking. And the summer went by.

They were afraid to meet. "Maybe, we won't like each other," each of them thought. They felt it was fine the way it was. The link between them grew much stronger than they would have imagined during their first conversations. They knew each other well. They hid nothing. Once, he told her that he had seen her on a bus. "How do I look?" she asked demurely.

"Wonderful," he said. "You have black, big eyes, chest-nut hair. . . . You are very tall. That is, not too much. Just the right height," he hastily added. "You have long, very long hair."

"No," she said, "I have hazel eyes. Blond hair. Short. Short. Very short. I'm five foot three."

He laughed. "Exactly." he said. He hadn't seen her. He was trying to visualize her. As for her, every time she gave a different description of herself. Finally, he would only ask: "Are you beautiful?"

"Very beautiful" she would answer. Then they stopped talking about that. He would like so much to see her. However, he didn't dare tell her. He was afraid of her beauty. Maybe, this time she had told him the truth. He refused to give a description of himself. He only said that he had blond hair, and that he was feeling old. Although he was only 34. He had married young. The kinds were growing up, and he felt he was a father with a lot of worries and responsibilities. He couldn't tell whether he would remarry. Perhaps, if he should meet a woman who would love him. And who would make a good mother for the kids.

Winter came. New Year's Eve was close. Everybody was making plans. He insisted that they should be together that night. She said no. She feared that the whole story would come to an end. She told him. He pondered. He told her he wasn't going any place without her. She decided to go to a party given by some friends.

He came up with a suggestion. On New Year's Eve he would stay home with the kids. He will put them to bed at about one o'clock. He would wait for her, and they would have a glass of champagne together. She didn't have to knock on the door. He would leave the door unlocked. She agreed.

It was a cold winter night. On New Year's Eve, after talking to him once more, she left. The party had started. She couldn't help thinking of what was going to happen. She didn't want to meet him. She was scared. At one o'clock she looked at her watch. She didn't feel like leaving. She was asked to dance. She kept thinking that he was waiting for her. "He must be impatient," she thought. "I wonder what he looks like." She was curious, but still scared. What if everything was just a lie? It couldn't be. His voice couldn't have deceived her. Why did she give her promise? She felt cheerful and sorry at the same time. The minutes flew. Once dance after another. She looked at her watch again. She couldn't make up her mind to leave. A mixture of fear of the unknown and fear of disenchantment was tormenting her. At three o'clock she suddenly made the decision. The next moment she was gone.

The name of the street... She forgot. She found the paper in her purse and read the address. Having paid the cab driver she stopped in front of the house for a few minutes. She pressed her coat closer. She was quivering with cold and fear. Music and voices were coming from the lighted windows. She couldn't hear his voice. She recognized the balcony. It was the fourth floor. Last window from the left. The other windows were facing another street. She looked at the lighted window. No shadow. She moved towards the stairs. She wanted to go up, and she felt she couldn't. The people were partying. She was climbing the stairs, one after another. She wouldn't take the elevator. She counted the stairs, hoping for her excitement to go away. And to stop shivering. To no avail, she found herself on the third floor. She waited for a while. Music was coming from an apartment. Someone could see her standing like this. She made it to his floor. She knew the door. The only one on the left side. She looked at the plate. She read his name. She slowly opened the door. She stopped in the foyer. Here, the light was off. From the next room, weak rays of a lamp were coming. She stood like this, for a time, noiseless. Nobody came to meet her. She entered the first room. There was no one. She saw the Van Gogh painting hanging where he had told her it was. She opened a door. He had told her, that was the children's room. It was dark. She went further into a small hall. She knew that it led to another room. She was moving quietly. Noiselessly. The door of the room was open. She didn't cross the threshold. It was quiet.

From the living room a few light beams were passing. She tried to see the room. With difficulty, she was able to perceive a shape in the bed. She heard a heavy, even breathing. He was asleep. Suddenly, a strange feeling came over her. She had only one thought; to run away. She moved back to the door. She closed it slowly. She made it to the street. For a few minutes, she ran as if somebody were chasing her. She didn't know why she was running this way. She took the first cab and went home. She disconnected the telephone. She had difficulty falling asleep.

THE WEDDING

Down there, in the valley, was a building site. Cattle stables were being built, or something of the sort. The workers didn't particularly care about the purpose of the construction. They only knew they were going to make it last, and it was to have a cement floor, and not be very tall; they knew a few other technical details. The building site wasn't too large, and the central office charged a single engineer with the supervision. Sure, he was young, quite young, but people liked him much, because he knew his job. When he said something, everyone knew it was going to come out well. His name was Paul. He was vague, dark-haired, had fine eyes and a quiet stare hidden at times behind glasses with so little corrective power that almost everyone thought they were worn just for the sake of wearing glasses. The glasses made him look soberer, more refined, that's what some people thought. Some chaps on the site would even order spectacles with their own "prescriptions" and sport them any time they had a date.

On the site, Paul was called "The Young One." He would address the older workers, or more mature ones, as "uncle." He was a warm person, and everyone liked him. People worked for his sake, or maybe, for the building site bonus. But they didn't talk about that. That's the way they were; they would rather talk about reasons having to do with heart.

Paul was the first to arrive at work. He used to say he was supposed to set an example, or that he would like to have one more look to see how the work was going.

One morning he found Dan at work. Dan was 21. He had had some schooling, but eventually he gave up, because his family wasn't that well off. His father had died in the war. The mother had taken care of him and his sister, Maria. His sister wasn't married yet, although the mother would push her to. She had several dates, because she was a nice girl, and a pretty one, but she didn't know whom to choose. She cared for no one in particular and the boys would say that she was uppity. As for Dan, he was a steadfast one. He loved a girl his age, and promised to marry her. All they were waiting for was for the girl to make herself a few dresses, a few bed sheets, and for both of them to have some money put aside, to be able to build a house for themselves.

"What's the matter, Dan, why are you here so early? It's hardly daybreak," Paul said.

"Nothing. Couldn't get a wink of sleep last night."

"C'mon, kid. Say, maybe you didn't sleep at home?"

"God forbid, I have never stayed away from home for the whole night. I just thought I'd better be an early bird this morning, 'cause today we get paid, and maybe I can get off a bit earlier."

"How's that, kid, to get off earlier?"

"I'm just saying. If there's no way, I won't."

The engineer checked the things around, had a look at the woodwork and made for the booth where he kept the blueprints. On his way he passed by Dan again. The engineer saw him looking in the mirror, he must have got something in his eye. When he saw the engineer he dropped the mirror.

"Bad omen," the engineer said laughing.

"My girlfriend's gonna leave me and I won't get married," Dan laughed back.

At seven everyone was at work. One could hear the even cadence of the carpenters fixing the stable roof. Dan was among them. All the way up on the top, he kept hammering rhythmically, along with the others.

The sun was getting fiery and dust was rising above the roof every time a truck drove by, carrying planks or other materials.

By lunch time the work stopped. However, Dan stayed to get done what he had started, because, as he used to say, one should never leave one's work half done, even if one's girl-friend was waiting. At that point, someone turned on a radio and loud music drowned out all conversation. In a corner, three workers must have been telling jokes, for they were roaring with laughter. Their laughter had a powerful, virile sound.

Suddenly all noise was silenced by a dreadful scream. The radio was turned off. For a moment everyone looked where the scream came from. Then, the people ran to the back of the new building. The engineer ran too; he had heard the scream from his booth. Next to a stone, in a pool of blood, lay Dan with his eyes closed and hands stretched out, as if on a cross. He seemed to utter some words, but nobody could understand them. He was the only one to know their meaning. While falling, he had been drawn by a strange fluid, sucking his will, and he had been hugged by something hot, hot as fire. Then he felt as weightless as a feather and saw himself being led away by his father, somewhere among the clouds.

"I meant to come to your wedding," the father said.

"But you will."

"No, I won't ever, because you'll never marry."

"Why do you say that, Father?"

"I had wanted to live, and to see you a bridegroom, Dan, do you hear me? Now, you are with me, you're not alive anymore, you must forget everything. You must forget Mother and Maria. You must forget your bride. If you won't, you'll be like me, wandering restlessly. A bullet got me when I was twenty-one, like yourself. You only know me from pictures. As I left for the front, you mother was carrying you in her womb. One day I got a letter saying I had a boy. I didn't get to see you when I was alive.

"But Father, I don't want to die! I don't want to ... I don't want ..."

As Dan opened his eyes he saw with dim sight the engineer's face. Then he saw nothing.

They took him to the hospital.

On the building site the work kept slowing down. As if the will to work had disappeared. Everyong was talking about the youth's accident. They were saying all kinds of things. Some were saying that the people who were next to him were at fault, because not everybody was down at once; others — that bad luck was haunting that place, and they'd better let everything go and work elsewhere. Still others knew for sure that no protective measures had been taken, and that the engineer was to be held responsible; but they wouldn't talk about that.

The engineer came to the site, casually looked about, without saying a word, and stood a minute, two, and more, next to the stone where the youth had been found. He experienced a tremendous feeling of remorse and knew that he was going to be sued. He knew that the investigation's findings would be against him. There were also a few bits of paper, all that silly stuff, proving that the building site manager had not approved the protection equipment fund, hell knows why. But all this didn't matter a whit.

Two days later, a peasant woman came to the site, wearing a black kerchief. A tiny, skinny woman with sad, scared eyes. She was Dan's mother. Next to her was a young girl blond-haired, with tears in her eyes. One could see that she was pregnant.

"What have you done to my boy?" the woman said, taking out a handkerchief. "Where is he?"

The engineer looked at her, then at the girl, then at her again. He couldn't utter a word. Feeling dizzy, he staggered toward the booth and beckoned the women to follow him.

"Your boy. . ." he muttered. He could say nothing else.

"What have you done to my boy?" the women lamented.

The young woman next to her wasn't crying anymore. She had big, frightened eyes, but something unseen and unknown seemed to give her power and hope.

"Don't cry, Mother," the young woman said.

"There," the mother went on, "Dan is going to have a baby. We were getting ready for the wedding."

The engineer could hardly utter the name of the hospital. The two women left. Next day, someone came from the hospital to give notice of Dan's death.

That day no one worked. The engineer disappeared and for quite a while nobody saw him. He ran to the woods, He was running between the trees, then he sat on a fallen log. He felt the earth turning, just like himself, but he wasn't afraid of the trail or jail. He was dominated instead by suffering and an obsessive vision. He thought he was seeing the youth dressed up in a black suit, laughing and offering him a glass of wine. Next to the youth was the bride in a white gown, leaning her willowy body on his shoulder. Dan would hug her, and then kick her in the womb. Paul awoke screaming and with a fever. He remembered the pregnant woman and Dan's mother. He had to give them some money.

Dan's funeral was attended by almost everyone who was working on the site. The engineer went as well, having advised the investigating panel where he was going. The village was a few miles from the site. Everyone in the village knew Dan's house — one could ask whomever one met. The mourning black cloth was hanging on the gate and a few elderly women were standing in front of the gate wailing and weeping. In the backyard the engineer found Dan's mother. He handed her the money, but the woman, bursting into tears said:

"You can't pay me for my boy. Not with all the gold in the world!"

Paul put the money on the table and left. On the threshold, he faced the young woman dressed in black. She fixed her eyes upon his, and a flow of hatred poured forth towards him. He lowered his eyes and went inside the house. He looked at Dan, and it seemed to him that the youth was smiling. He heard a sonorous laughter, and he thought he heard someone shouting: "Long live the bride and bridegroom!" He saw Dan in the middle of the crowd, dancing. The bride's white veils were floating by him, wraping him up, so that he couldn't be seen anymore. The bride was the only one to be seen, there in the midst of the people, and the veils which were slithering and floating along with the movements of the dance.

Dan's girlfriend made her appearance on the threshold, again. Paul faced her eyes once more, as inflexible, as full of sorrow as before.

Paul found himself running down the highway towards the building site. The night fell. There was only the night guard on the site. Paul made for the spot of the accident. On the ground next to the stone which had killed Dan, was a mirror. Surely, it was the youth's mirror, but it remained unbroken.

THE NIGHT OF THE RISING DEAD
(*Edited by Robert Lyle*)

I

Large snowflakes covered the streets. It was the first snow of the year and it seemed to embody the power of all new beginnings. Everything was white. The sidewalks, the cars parked along the curbs. The little sidewalk kiosks. Night was coming. In the winter, the night comes early. And fast. Alex was staring out the window of Maria's apartment. The street lights made the flakes sparkle. Actually, it was the street lights which made the flakes visible. Alex watched. They descended, by the thousands. But slowly.

"Do you know what I was doing at three o'clock this morning?"

Maria didn't hear him as she walked into the room.

"Why are you sitting here in the dark?" she asked.

"Maria! Do you know what I was doing at three a.m.?"

"You were sleeping," she said as she turned a lamp on and sat on the sofa.

Absentmindedly, she thumbed through the pages of a magazine.

Alex continued to gaze out of the window.

"I was talking to you last night."

"In your dream," she answered, not looking up.

"No. In reality. I was talking to you."

"And what were we talking about? I seem to have forgotten," she said, giving Alex a very sweet smile.

"About Einstein's theory of relativity."

"What," she laughed.

"Imagine if we could reach the speed of light. Suppose we could travel at that speed for an hour. Far, far into outer space. Far from earth. And then return. We would only be gone an hour. But the earth would have aged one hundred years. A century would have passed. Familiar faces would have disappeared. Old places gone. Life would probably be very different. The houses, the pace of life itself, perhaps new ideas — deeper ones. But we, the space travelers, would still be young. And we could go on living for another hundred years. Wouldn't that be fantastic!"

Maria sat with the open magazine, but had stopped reading.

Look at his face, she thought, the face of a young man. But in many years, he's going to be like any other old man.

"It would be wonderful if we could live hundreds of years," she said aloud. "But only if we could stay young. Do you think that might be possible some day?"

"Who knows. But why not. Stories have always been told about a fountain of youth. But then those stories are just that — myths and legends."

"If we could travel at the speed of light, we could leave and come back every hour. Every hundred years."

"Would you like to live in outer space?"

"Why not?"

"Maria, this whole thing about traveling at the speed of light is just mathematical theory. Abstraction. In truth, of course, we live within a very absolute time. The one we've got here on earth. Sure, it would be nice to stay young. If I really got to choose, I think I'd stop at thirty."

"Suppose you could travel at the speed of light into space. Would you go without me?"

Alex walked to the sofa and sat next to Maria, lowering his face to hers.

"Silly girl," he said softly.

They remained silent for a moment. But Maria couldn't stop thinking about the possibilities.

"Do you think there are already flying saucers out there which can reach the speed of light?"

"I don't think. I'd like to think there are. That they come from superior civilizations on other planets. Different from our earth. And that we could communicate with them and even work together for the betterment of all mankind."

"You sound like a poet, not an architect. You spend more time thinking about outer space than you do about building's."

"Oh, I'm always thinking about buildings. You know, ever since I was a little kid, I dreamed about designing a house to look like a flying saucer — circular, suspended in the air. Supported by some invisible power. It would have large windows. It would turn so that its solar panels could follow the sun. But now, well, ... I don't want to think about buildings. I was thinking about that TV program on flying saucers. And that photograph."

"Yes, I saw that."

"You did? You used to say that was all fantasy. But now — well, I think it's fascinating. That picture seemed to show some kind of material bodies. Nobody knew what they really were — mysterious figures, stars, cosmic objects of some sort. Whatever they are, I don't think you can rule out the possibility of their being from other planets. After all, human fantasy begins with a question mark. Why shouldn't we dream and wonder, looking at photographs we cannot comprehend? Why shouldn't we imagine some kind of astro-people, born out of electrical fields in the voids of space, made of bunches of antennas, communicating through microwaves, or having other miraculous powers? Who knows, perhaps they know the secret of eternal youth? Wouldn't it be great to meet them?

"What if they took over the earth?"

"We could come to an agreement. They must be intelligent. They might be good and beautiful and reject war. We could greet them with smiles and flowers. And offer them our most advanced ideas. They might be more rational than we, while we could teach them about love. About the beauties of a symphony or of a flower."

"How do you know that the people of earth wouldn't simply wage war on these strangers from outer space. We know how to hate and kill too."

"Not us."

"Maybe not you and me, but many people do. And in the end, we would all be responsible."

"My little wise girl," Alex smiled as he kissed her hand. "You're right. On the other hand, however, it might just happen that powerful light from the great beyond might one day shine to earth and all the people here would unite and greet it."

"I've always known that you were a dreamer," she said. "You studied in school just for its mystery. I think you should have been a science fiction writer."

It was pitch dark outside now and the large flakes continued to fall, driven to earth by a new intensity.

II

Maria's father was frequently away for long intervals on his job and she and her mother often invited Alex to stay for dinner. This evening, the meal-time conversation soon returned to the great unknown.   "You know, mother, Alex was saying how fascinating it would be to be able to travel at the speed of light, far into outer space."

"That's too fast for me. Anyway, it won't happen anytime soon."

"Unfortunately," said Alex, "it'll never happen to me. Even if it came soon enough, I'm too weak."

"Oh, I wish you could do it," Maria said, laughing.

"Wish me good health. That's all anyone needs," Alex answered in a suddenly somber mood.

"Are you afraid of death?" she asked.

"No. Well, not afraid, but I know I'm going to die when I'm thirty. But look at the bright side, I'll always be young. At least in people's memories."

Maria's mother looked surprised, but said nothing. She went to the kitchen.

Alex had gotten up and walked to the couch. Maria followed and sat beside him.

"What are you talking about? Why did you say you'd die at thirty?"

"Never mind. I just know I'm going to die at thirty."

Maria stroked his cheek.

"Stop talking nonsense. Why should you die?"

"It's not nonsense. For many years I've known that I was going to die at thirty. You'll see. I know it."

"I call this all nonsense. Talking about youth and death in the same breath. You know my girlfriend, Victoria. I don't know if you knew, but she once had a brother. His name was Christian and when he was 26, he went away to the war. He was at the front for a long, long time. And he saw and experienced and faced death many times in many ways. But he survived and came home alive and well when the war was over. Let me show you his picture."

Maria found the old photograph in a drawer and handed it to Alex.

He gasped and turned pale, but said nothing.

"He was very handsome," said Maria. "Victoria has often said so. I never saw him, though. Anyway, he came home from the war and everybody was happy. He was the only son, the only brother, and he came back alive and well. He was happy and outgoing as ever, although Victoria says that once in a while he would remember something and his eyes would grow dark with some obsessive thought."

"Two months after he came home, he met a girl. Her name was Adriana and she was beautiful. She was young and beautiful and kind. It was the first time he had ever fallen in love. All the tense, blood-filled days and the frightful nights of the war seemed to have done one thing — given him an immeasurable capacity of love."

"The heavy memories tormented him," she said.

"After awhile, they were married and she soon became pregnant. But the child died before it was born; he took Adriana to the hospital and they performed surgery, but it was no use. Adriana got an infection."

"Christian took her home to their small room — it wasn't far from here, as a matter of fact — but she never recovered. She died a few days later."

"Christian took her in his arms; he didn't cry, he just pressed her against his chest, repeating 'my little girl, I'll warm you up!'"

"For many hours he would not let go of her. Finally his parents and in-laws came and managed to put her into a coffin, but Christian would not leave her side."

"When they were ready to take her to the cemetery, he clung to the coffin and said, 'I'll always be with you'.

"He went to the cemetery every day, but in two months he fell ill and quickly died. He died because he wanted to die.

"It was then that the dark moments of the war stuck in his mind, more real than ever, because of his Adriana's death.

"Well," continued Maria, "Victoria loved her brother so much that she kept saying, 'I shall die at 27'. That's how she really felt because she didn't think she could survive his death. But she's thirty now — and she's very much alive."

Maria looked at Alex, but he did not respond. His head was bowed and he was pale.

"Forgive me for making you sad. I don't know why I told you that story. I just wanted you to give up that thought of death. Sometimes we think we will die soon; maybe it's just the idea that fascinates us; maybe we expect the whole world to weep at our death. I guess we forget that everyone forgets everything — even the things which shouldn't be forgotten."

Maria came close to Alex and kissed him.

"I've got to leave now," said Alex. "It's late."

The young man rose, put his coat on and spoke to Maria's mother who had just re-entered the room.

"Good night, Mrs. Barton, thank you."

Maria walked him to the door.

"Don't be sad," she said. "Forgive me?"

I'm not mad, Maria. Why should I be?"

He kissed her good night and left.

Maria walked back to the dining room where her mother stood holding Christian's photograph.

"Maria. What is this photograph?"

"Oh, that's Victoria's brother. I showed it to Alex."

"How could you, Maria? Don't you see how much this picture looks like Alex?"

"You're right!" said Maria. "That's why he grew so sad. They look exactly alike."

Mrs. Barton went to her own room, leaving Maria pondering the photograph.

"Did Victoria tell you why she was going to be late?" Mrs. Barton called back.

III

Maria opened up her bed and turned off the light.

She tried to go to sleep, but the thoughts wouldn't let her. Her mind was tortured by both reality and imagination.

The questions intermingled. The visions switched.

She tried to follow a thought, to find its meaning. But it was useless.

She turned her face to the wall. But she could not fall asleep. In a violent moment, she threw the blanket off. It was hot. But it ony seemed hot because without the cover, it was cold. She covered herself again.

Thoughts — again, and again, visions.

She got out of bed and looked from the window. The large flakes were still falling. It was the first snow this year and already it had covered everything. The houses were dressed in white.

On a neighboring balcony, Maria noticed a bird. It was all snuggled down in with snow on top of it. Once in awhile, the bird would move its wings and the snow would slip off.

"Why does this bird stay here, waiting to be covered by snow? What does it do? It doesn't sleep. Could it possibly be watching the snowfall? What kind of bird is it — it looks like a sparrow.

"Do birds think? I heard they do, and so do animals. how do they think? What do they think about? If I make a sign, will it see me?"

Maria put her hand to the window, gently spreading her fingers out. The bird did not move. Maria moved her hand across the glass. The bird remained immobile. It did not hear her.

Maria moved way from the window. She wanted to sleep. It was so late. she looked at her watch. It was past midnight. Tomorrow is a working day, she thought, and I have to get up at seven as usual.

She knew she'd be late again in the morning, rushing to get to the studio just before eight.

Maybe it will still be snowing. As lovely as now. But even if it is, she thought, she would have to stay in the middle of that paint smell.

What would she paint tomorrow? Today, she had been painting pictures of brown bears, almost life size. What do they need them for anyway, she thought. Oh well, they're for schools, for science classes. She would do her best. The children deserve it.

At their age, they should see only lovely things and have only kind people around. There's plenty of time to learn about life's problems, worries, hardships. Tomorrow, it might be a butterfly.

She would make it sparkle, with wide-spread wings. It will be suspended in air, and underneath there will be a red flower. The butterfly will be watching it. It won't be watching any other flowers or grasses or weeds. I'll make the loveliest butterfly in the world.

Maria layed back down, but she could not sleep. She lighted the lamp. Victoria's bed sat there untouched. Who knows what kept her, Maria thought. She took a book from the shelf and opened it. The letters ran against her eyes.

> *To be, or not to be? that is the question:*
> *Whether 'tis nobler in the mind to suffer*
> *The slings and arrows of outrageous fortune,*
> *Or to take arms against a sea of troubles,*
> *And by opposing, end them? To die; to sleep. . .*

"No," she said. "It's no good reading this now. I can't read about death at night." She put the book away, turned off the light and layed facing the wall. There's a noise. Someone's at the door. They're trying to turn the key, but it doesn't work. But, of course! It's Victoria. She just can't make her key work.

Maria jumped out of bed and unlocked the door. The door flew open. She jumped back. Her eyes were frightened and she turned pale.

"Alex," she whispered.

The young man, supported by Victoria came into the room and Maria took his arm. Alex's face was pale and drawn. He was frightened. He had a black eye. The girls took him to the bed. Victoria ran to the bathroom and returned with a wet towel. Maria wiped the blood from his face.

"What happened?" Maria asked.

"I found him in front of the building. He was lying unconscious in the snow," Maria answered.

Alex just stared at Victoria.

"Alex, what happened?" Maria asked. "Didn't you go home?"

"I did," Alex answered in a faint whisper.

Maria's mother, awakened by the activity, came into the room and helped comfort the youth.

"Victoria!"Alex stared at the young woman intensely. "Your brother called on me tonight."

No one spoke. Victoria frowned.

"What are you talking about," Maria finally asked with irritation. "Where did you get these bruises?"

"I fell," he said. "It's true. Victoria's brother came to me tonight.

"I left here and went straight home and to bed. I fell asleep quickly. Suddenly, a voice woke me up. A voice calling my name.

"I opened my eyes, but it was dark. I closed them again, but I couldn't sleep. Soon, I heard the voice again. Only this time it was very close.

"It said something in my ear, but I couldn't understand. I heard a swish, but I was too frightened to open my eyes. A cold breath of air touched my face. Then, somebody whispered:

"'Don't be frightened. It's me, Victoria's brother, Christian. You heard my story tonight. You've seen me; I'm your mirrow image. Open your eyes and look at me.'

"I didn't open my eyes, but I said;

"'What do you want with me. You're dead. What are you doing in this world?'

"'Don't be afraid!' he said. 'Don't. Open your eyes. I'm just like you — your copy, your soul. Look at me!'

Again, I felt the cold breath. I felt it over my entire body. I tried to pull the blanket over my head, but someone pulled it aside.

"'Wake up', the voice said.

"'I am wide awake.'

"'Open your eyes.'

"I slowly opened my eyes. I didn't move. The room was pitch dark. I couldn't see anything. I got up and picked it up from the floor. I wrapped it around myself. I was cold. I went to turn on the light. But something — a power — stopped me.

"The voice said: 'don't turn on the light. You must see me.'

"I shouted: 'What do you want? Where are you?'

"'I'm in front of you. Look.'

"In the dark, I could distinguish the shape of a man. It was a vague form. Transparent. White and transparent, like the photographic negative. It moved. It's body bent. I could see his face. It was grey and transparent as well. Like smoke, like nothingness, like an illusion, like uncertainty itself.

"Now and then, he would disappear. Only his eyes, strangely, stayed on. The eyes were colored. Yes, they were colored. They watched me closely, persistently, glass cold. I've never seen such eyes.

"There was a strange beauty to them. They were violet, large and bright. I can still see them.

"I was fascinated. I cried out; 'What wonderful eyes!'

"For a few moments, we watched each other. We said nothing. But I became irritated and asked again.

"'Who are you and what do you want?'

"'I told you. I'm Victoria's brother, Christian. I died before I was 27. You ask why I've come. I've been looking for a long time for someone like me. Just like me.

"'Not only do you look like me, but you have a peculiar wish — to die young so that people will always remember you the way you are now.'

"'What a naive thought. Do you really think people remember? And if they do, for how long? Death kills memory. But if you want, I can give you the opportunity to have your wish.'

"'It's simple. I want to live. I want to exist! Let's make a deal.'

"Alex answered: 'You died because you were in love.'

"'Perhaps. Perhaps I died because I loved people. Because I had seen people dying all around me. My friends died and I couldn't help them live. My sweetheart died. I couldn't do anything to prevent the people I loved from dying. What could be more precious than life!'

"'You have life and yet you keep saying that you are going to die at thirty. Why? Why should you die? Do you know what is beyond life? I'll tell you. Sorrow. Only sorrow. Sorrow for not being able to exist. Sorrow for not having lived enough. I want to live! Let's switch places.'

"'No, I don't want to die,' I cried out. 'I don't want to.'

"But he wouldn't leave me alone.

"'You don't want to die? But what do you do to keep death away? To defend life?'

"'What if the dead were to avenge themselves? What if the dead, all the dead, we, the young ones killed against our will by stupid human ambition and shortsightedness, what if we take life? What will be left of your earth then? And those like you, who have everything, but do nothing to defend it, who do not love light? You, You will die at thirty! You are so petty. Defend your soul. Do something for your conscience. In our name!'

"Those eyes came very close to me, sparkling. The cold breath brushed my face and froze my soul. I wanted to LIVE, more than anything.

"'Think well. If you really want to die when you are young, switch with me. Nobody will know. Think about it. As for me, I want daylight; I hate this darkness!'

"And he was gone. He disappeared. I ran out the door and down the street. Somehow I got here. I think I fell, but I'm not sure what happened. I remember running up the street."

IV

The smell of paint permeated the studio. The girls in front of easels, painting butterflies today.

"What kind of butterfly is that?" asked Maria.

"Oh, just a butterfly," Victoria answered.

"It's not just a butterfly. But anyway, I don't think you're supposed to be painting it that color."

"Maybe we need butterflies this color too."

"Victoria, don't play games. We're supposed to be painting these white against a blue background."

"There are butterflies that are other colors."

"Sure there are, but that's not what we're supposed to be painting."

"Why not? Other colored butterflies exist, so we should paint them too — white butterflies, colored butterflies, black butterflies, dead-head butterflies."

Maria did not respond and Victoria fell silent. Only the slight swish of their brushes could be heard for some time.

"Maria, do you believe Alex's story?"

"I don't know what to think. I'd say he probably just had a nightmare."

"Alex is a dreamer, Maria. That's where he really resembles Christian. Sensitive. Romantic. Inspired."

The day passed quickly in the artist loft where the two girls turned out paintings used primarily in school rooms. Butterflies. Birds. Full of life.

It was late in the day when Alex climbed the stairs to the studio.

"Alex, how do you feel, darling," Maria asked, walking to greet him

"Not bad, except that bruise still hurts a little."

"Don't worry, it will go away. What time is it, anyway."

"Time to go home. I came to pick you up. It's past five."

"Are you coming, Victoria?" Maria asked, turning to her friend who had barely looked up from her painting.

"No, I'm going to stay for awhile."

Alex walked to the easel where Victoria continued to be deeply absorbed. He looked for a long time at Victoria's butterfly. His face made a strong expression.

The butterfly seems to have very heavy wings. And it is flying, very, very, slowly, he thought.

Then there's Victoria. She looks so pale today. And she's so quiet, he thought.

"Are you going to be home soon?" Maria asked as she slipped her arm into her coat.

"As soon as I finish," Victoria answered without looking up.

Maria and Alex walked through the snow, at first not saying much.

"Victoria was very impressed by your story last night."

"Why do you call it a story? Didn't you believe me?"

"I don't know, Alex. I think you're awfully tired. Maybe you should stay at our apartment tonight. You can stay in the guest room and you'll get a good rest. That's what you need. You're too alone at your place."

"We'll see. There's a lot of evening left."

V

The snow had stopped falling. It was cold, though, and the snow squeaked under foot. People were lingering in front of shop windows, but they hurried when passing through deserted sections of the streets and alleys.

Alex and Maria parted a few blocks from the studio. He had told her he had something to take care of at home. He didn't really. He just told her that he wasn't sure he had locked his door. Hardly convincing.

Whether Maria believed it or not didn't matter. What mattered was that Alex wanted to walk alone, watching the people, feeling the frost, listening to the remote sounds of music.

His steps were taking him — he couldn't tell why, exactly — to isolated spots. He went into a bar, looking for — he didn't know what. The noise, the crowd, the smoke was too much.

A movie. Yes, a movie. A comedy would do it, he thought. But ten minutes into the film, he left. It was not fun.

He walked first in one direction. Then abruptly turned around. The thoughts kept bothering him. Upsetting. Obsessing him.

His steps took him into the large park in the center of the city, toward the lake. An icy, sharp wind cut through to his very insides. He walked more slowly.

Where am I headed? he wondered. I don't know. It's dark.

Alex remembered the white shadow and thought for a moment he could see it again under the ice crust on the lake. He stopped and looked again, but there was nothing there. Just the smoke-like vapor of his breath.

If I see the shadow again I won't be scared, he thought. Those eyes, so alive and fascinating. Alive and penetrating. Alive and sad. Such a deep sadness. And a desire coming through with incredible brilliance.

It was late and he was very alone. He and his thoughts.

I'd like to see those eyes again. I'd like to hear that deep, muffled voice of that man. Man? Can I think of that shadow as a man.

Alex remembered the previous night and how he felt. The strange presence before actually seeing it. How he was so startled, but that his fear had turned to some strange emotion. He was sure those eyes had told him many things. A lot more than words. He just wasn't sure what.

It was freezing, dark and lonely. Suddenly, Alex remembered that he had promised Maria he would come to her apartment. He hurried off. He was going to keep his promise.

VI

Alex arrived as they were finishing dinner. Victoria was there too.

"I called father today," Maria told everyone. "He said he is going to be home in a couple of days. He's working very hard. That's how it is at the end of the year. Oh, Alex, mother says you are welcome to stay here tonight."

"Thanks, but, uh, I don't want to inconvenience you."

"It's no trouble, Alex," answered Maria's mother. "We'd feel better having a man in the house, anyway. My dear husband works so hard. We have to stay by ourselves so often."

Alex did not hear. His eyes had met Victoria's and it seemed as if she was trying to say something.

Her eyes are so sad, he thought. She's very weary. And thoughtful.

Victoria did not utter a word, but Alex felt as if she wanted to say, "No, don't stay."

Mrs. Barton went into the guest room to make up the spare bed for Alex while Maria cleared the table.

Alex sat in an armchair and Victoria, still preoccupied, went to the window.

Abruptly, she turned and looked at Alex, but said nothing. She stared at him. Intently. From just a few feet away, she watched him.

The young man was taken aback by Victoria's uneasing gaze. She seemed to want to learn something.

Alex blushed — he didn't know why — and whispered;
"I shouldn't stay, should I?"

The young woman did not hear him. Or at least she
didn't want to acknowledge that she heard him. Without a
word, she turned and left the room.

For a few moments, Alex sat alone. He had felt something strange in Victoria's stare. Something which sent
shivers down his spine. But something which made him wish
he could talk to her.

Perhaps we have the same thoughts, the same feelings,
he thought.

"It's time to turn in," said Maria, as she entered the
living room. "I'm tired and I need a good nights rest."

"Should I stay?" Alex asked, almost sure he should have
just left.

"But of course," Maria answered, in a very firm voice.

Tired from the previous night and the long walk he had
taken earlier in the evening, Alex fell asleep quickly. Everyone was asleep; only Victoria tossed and turned in her bed
from time to time.

It was quiet. Outside, the snow began to fall again and
the night's darkness was diluted by the dim sparkling of the
flakes falling to earth.

Midnight. The apartment was deep in sleep, but Victoria
got out of bed. Noiselessly. Her steps were small and quiet.
Her feet hardly touched the floor. Her long, white gown
floated about her body. With hardly a sound, she unlocked
the door and glided down the stairs.

"I have come," she said as she removed her hairpins and
shook her hair loose, walking out into the snowy night.

Her long hair fell down over her shoulders. A slight
breeze pressed the gown against her body, making every line
apparent. The snow stroked her face. The flakes clung to her
hair.

"You called me," she said in a low voice.

Amid the flakes, a face appeared. It was like a white
smoke, and two penetrating eyes stared at her. They seemed
immobile, yet sparkling, alive. Flaming.

Victoria's eyes watched. The wind gently swirled the
snow about her. Her bare feet were covered by the soft snow.

"I called you. I knew you would come." The low voice was one she recognized.

"I suggested to Alex that we trade places. Has he made up his mind? Make him decide — quickly!"

"I don't think he has decided. But why even ask him —just do it."

"I can't, alone. Only by all of us in this world, joining together — joining our wills together — could we come back to earth. Then it would be all of us."

"So why don't you all come back?"

"Why? Because we do not want to sacrifice all the living — our brothers and sisters and parents and friends — we cannot sacrifice them all so that we can live."

"I would gladly give my life."

"Individually, we can only trade places with someone who is not our own flesh and blood. I can only take the place of a person who looks just like me. But the blood must be different. He must be strong and young. But he cannot know much about us. He must agree. That is the law of our night."

"When you died, a lot of people hardly noticed. Some remembered, for awhile. But they soon forgot. Why should you care what happens to them?"

"We have a huge power. Power far beyond what men can even imagine. If we join our forces, the darkest, the brightest night, would fall over the earth."

For a moment, Victoria could imagine the catastrophe. People, those she knew well. People she worked with. Her friends. Their faces yellow, their bodies lifeless on the ground. A shiver passed through her body and she seemed to come out of her trance-like state.

Could that really happen she thought. Is it already decided? Can anything be done?

"How can people prevent that night?"

"There's only one way," the voice responded. "People must be aware of us. Ignorance is not bliss. They must know us. Then, they must forget their differences. They must work together because their will can overcome ours.

"Make Alex decide," the voice pleaded.

They eyes grew dim and flickered, like embers, against the horizon. The voice was thicker — it became a call:

"Otherwise, I'll bring our wills together. Decide, or the darkest, the brightest night will come."

The eyes flared brightly and the light reflected in Victoria's eyes. She felt dizzy, but strangely full of life. She was shivering.

"I'm so cold," she cried weakly.

The shadow faded and disappeared. She felt blows striking her everywhere. The pain was in every part of her body. Her eyes sparkled for a moment. Then she collapsed.

In the morning, a passerby found her lying in the snow in front of the building.

VII

The physician was vague. Victoria had a fever, a high fever. She was restless, and did not recognize anyone. She tossed and turned from side to side. She was asleep, but not asleep.

"It was that story of yours that made her sick, Alex," Maria said in a tone that Alex knew he should not answer. He only felt guilty.

"The night is coming, the night is coming," were the only words Victoria would mumble from time to time. Nothing else. Just, "the night is coming."

Maria tried to gently question her, but to no avail.

The doctor came in and administered a sedative and Victoria's face grew calmer. She lay, face up, with her eyes closed. Perhaps she was sleeping.

But every once in a while, she would repeat, almost imperceptably:

"The night is coming."

Two days passed and Victoria remained gravely ill. She spoke to no one. The doctor brought more doctors for consultations, but they could not find the cause. "Perhaps, it's just a nervous breakdown," suggested one.

Victoria stared at the ceiling, fixing on some distant point. Maria tried to talk to her, but her friend would not answer. Just, now and then, she would say, as if an automation:

"The night is coming."

VII

As the harshest days of winter began to wane, the sun came out full. It was still freezing and the snow remained firm. Victoria was fine now, although in her dream she could remember her "obsession" as Maria called it. In her dreams she could hear her own voice saying: "the night is coming." But the girls did not dwell on it.

Alex's strange story had pretty much been forgotten. The sun, even when it is cold, awakens dreams of spring. The newspapers were filled with stories about UFO's and how they could not possibly be real.

Alex always felt sad when anyone made fun of flying saucers. After all, he thought, those denials do not rely on any serious investigation. Maybe, just maybe, he thought, we do have visitors from outer space. And even if we don't, it would be fascinating to go to other galaxies and other planets and look for them.

Alex had been invited to dinner at the Barton's and had stopped at the studio to pick up Maria.

"Hi," he said as he crossed the threshold. "Thought I'd come to take you home."

"That's nice," she said, cleaning her brushes.

"Victoria didn't come to work today?" Alex asked, noticing her easel was empty.

"Yes, she did. She went to show a sketch around. It was very strange, very sohpisticated. I couldn't understand it, I don't even know what it is."

"Is she all right?"

"I think so. She doesn't complain. Except... at night, she keeps talking in her sleep."

Just then Victoria returned to the studio, but insisted that Alex and Maria go ahead.

"I'm going to stay for just a little while longer," she said, apologizing for having kept them.

"Oh, come on," said Maria. "Father is home and it's a special dinner."

"Oh, all right. I'll hurry. You go ahead and I'll catch up."

"Hurry then."

Maria's father greeted Alex in his usual way. "Hi, Sonny. How are you? Still Dreaming?"

"How's the job?" replied Alex.

"Lots of work and no complaints."

Maria went to help her mother in the kitchen, leaving the two men alone.

Maria's father asked Alex about the "story" he had told the girls months before Victoria's illness.

"She's so delicate," Mr. Barton said. "The sad case of that poor brother of hers. That story you told must have awaken memories that were just too strong for her and it knocked her out. Lucky thing she got well, poor kid."

Alex gritted his teeth, then said: "I don't think I had a nightmare. I'm convinced it really happened."

"What!!!"

"It did — exactly as I told them that night. Didn't they tell you?"

"Sure they did. But, come on Sonny Boy, who do you think you're kidding? Do I look like the kind of fool who would believe that stuff? Sure, there are things one shouldn't forget. And above all, which should never happen again. But . . ."

"Why didn't you come home when Maria called you and told you what had happened. When Victoria became so ill?"

"Well, ... I couldn't. I didn't want to mention it to the girls, but . . . well, a young fellow fell from the scaffolding to his death the day she called."

"What?" Alex exploded in surprise.

His mind raced. That was the day after he had met Christian. Before Victoria was found in the snow. Could there be a connection?

"Sad. He was young, too. Twenty-two or twenty-three at most. Sad. Very sad."

They remained silent for a moment, but Maria's father broke the quiet.

"Let's talk about something more cheerfull. Hey, where are the girls? Maria!"

"Coming."

Maria wanted to turn on the light, but her father said it was a bity early for that.

"It's winter, it still gets dark early," she said.

Maria walked to the window and notice how dark it was already getting.

"It might snow again," she said to no one in particular.

Suddenly, the sky grew very dark. A wind, a strange, powerful wind suddenly picked up in the street. It was loud. Very loud.

Alex and Maria's father jumped up and joined her at the window.

"What could it be," he asked.

No one answered. Or even tried. The wind grew fierce. It was dark, but the street lights were not on.

"The light doesn't work," said Mrs. Barton as she joined them at the window.

"Let's light some candles," said Maria.

"Wait," said her father, "there's no need. This will pass quickly and then it will lighten up again."

Windows and doors slamming and banging could be heard. The wind continued to grow stronger and stronger. Things were lifted from the ground and then thrown back to the earth. A piece of tin roofing clanged to the street. Noises were becoming overwhelming.

Victoria was trying to run down the street, but she could barely move against the wind. Traffic had slowed to a crawl, and then virtually stopped. She clung to a fence, then inched her way with enormous effort to a building wall. Only one thought filled her mind; I want to get home.

She knew why it was so dark.

Some people tried to run on the streets — in all directions. But the wind only got stronger. And it started to snow. Harder and harder. The darkness was total. Noise was everywhere and the wind simply amplified it. Metal and wood thrown to the earth, broken windows and people crying.

Victoria felt the frozen flakes stinging her cheeks. She tried to run, but new blows stopped her. Her breathing was heavy and it became harder and harder to move at all.

Suddenly, the wind shifted direction and it was at her back. She ran, she flew before the wind. She was sweating now, so she dropped her coat.

She ran and ran. The important thing was to get home. She could not see an inch in front of her face, but she kept running. It was total darkness, all around.

She found herself in front of the building. I must get upstairs. Home, she thought. I must tell them how they can overcome the darkness, how we can overcome it. Overcome this pitch darkness that is dominating the world. All it takes is for us to forget our differences, to work together, she thought.

She stumbled and clawed her way up the stairs and rang the bell. No answer. The bell didn't work.

She pounded on the door with her last bit of energy. "It's me, Victoria."

The door opened and the girl repeated: "It's me, Victoria. Listen to me. The night is coming. We must unite, only united can we overcome the darkness."

She took one more breath and collapsed to the floor.

The building began to shake, as if from an earthquake, and the earth itself seemed to be splitting apart. Human voices disappeared. Bricks and windows, stones and boards, flew in a swirl. Above the tremendous noise, one voice — Victoria's penetrated the boiling mass, the walls and gates. It entered easily the glass windows. It said on and on:

"Only united can we drive away the darkness."

COLORS

Every day I walked next to people. I watched them. Often, I stopped to admire the velvety complexion of a young girl, the warm smile a mother gave her little one, the smooth, rich hair of a blond youth, the self-assured walk of a passer-by in a hurry, the lithe profile of a ballerina or the energetic hand of a man holding his balance in a bus. But people I worked with — I thought of them in terms of their work. I forgot that people were people. Sometimes I associated them with machines.

That's how things were. Simple. No doubts, no complications. No problems. Up to a day. There was a free seat in a bus. In the front section. A man was sitting in the seat opposite of me. I don't know what he looked like. I couldn't see his face. I saw a pair of large eyes and I forgot what I was doing. Those eyes sparkled. They threw two bands of light into my eyes. All of a sudden, they grew red. Red as fire. I had difficulty getting off the bus. I left. The eyes, filled with fire, were following me. I looked back. They weren't there. Day after day I looked for them. I was looking for that burning fire. I was looking for the spirit of a man whose sight was illuminated by sunshine. I was looking for its sparkling light. I watched people's eyes. I watched carefully. Then I realized that people's eyes were colored. Lots of colors. Lots of shades. I saw some eyes, blue as a clear spring sky. I saw green eyes, like fresh dewey grass. I saw yellow eyes, like ripe sheaves of wheat. I saw grey eyes, like the ashes of burned-down trees. I saw pink eyes, like rosebuds. But those eyes, red as sun, I couldn't find them. I watched people. And no longer could I see them as objects or machines. I looked at them, and their eyes told me of their souls. Each of those people had a soul that I could now easily see, because I could tell the color of their eyes. I saw lots of clear-colored eyes. Many sparkled reminescent of sky colors. Or grass. Or stars. young trees.

Sturdy mountains. Years passed by while I looked for those red eyes. In the meantime, I found thousands of other eyes. Soul's eyes.

One day, just a day like any other, but yet a new, sunny day, I was hiking in the mountains, as I did every Sunday. Then, in front of me, going downhill, a pair of black eyes appeared. Black as pitch. Sad as nothingness. They stopped in front of me. Wonder. The black eyes grew red. The black eyes were the red eyes. The black eyes were "my" eyes. The eyes I was looking for. The eyes that taught me to see the human being. The eyes that gave me the restlessness of being happy. I wondered, why were those black eyes going downhill? And they told me: because we thought that sky-blue eyes were down there. We looked at each other, and again, the black eyes sent me two light rays. We used no words. Our minds embraced. And we set off together to the top of the mountain.

THE WISH

Diana decided to stay home. As soon as Eddy left for his business trip she picked up the phone and called her friend Andra. However, she couldn't find her either in the consultation room or in the emergency room. She left a message asking her friend to call back and after only a few minutes she heard the soft ring.

"Anything wrong?" Andra asked with concern.

Diana was pregnant, and Andra started worrying whenever she would get a call from her.

"No, nothing wrong," Diana said with a smile. "I'm just missing you. How about stopping by?"

"I'm a little bit tired, I was in charge of the emergency room last night. However, I'll drop in to see you."

Before leaving the hospital Andra would usually make a tour of the newborn clinic. She would stop by each baby, have a careful look, smile at those who seemed more playful, and then she would leave. That day, as usual, she went to the locker room, and started changing. She put on her blue wool outfit, combed her hair. Now, her outlook was totally different.

It was five o'clock. She was looking forward to having a nice, at least one-hour long talk with Diana.

Andra had divorced her husband about five years before. It hadn't been her fault. Her ex had simply left one day for the hospital and never come back. It hurt horribly. The time, since then, has somewhat relieved her pain, her love for him and her loneliness.

Diana met Andra at the door, with her usual, open smile; she looked happy and was holding a bunch of white carnations.

"What's the matter?" Andra marveled.

"Two events. First, I read your article in the medical journal. Second, I saw the TV report on your successful infertility treatment."

"Isn't this really touching," Andra said laughing, "I never heard of any entertainer reading medical journals."

"I read plenty of medical journals right now. And look at all these books Eddy's got for me: *How to Care for Your New Baby* and *Mother and Her Baby*. Well, how's that?"

"Excellent. How's the little one, growing fast, huh?" Andra said while arranging her jacket on a chair.

The two friends laughed.

"You're making it, aren't you," Diana said after a short while; she was watching her friend and she was thinking that Andra looked extremely pretty and young.

"Just incredible, considering how hard she works," Diana concluded.

"Let me tell you the good news: I'll be defending my Ph.D. soon."

"That's wonderful. What the subject?"

"Sterility, of course. I really wish that every woman who feels like having a child could have one."

"It's wonderful, having children," Diana agreed. "Although, I really think that a career is more important."

Andra gave her a sad look and said:

"You're wrong. A woman must be a mother. However, what is really the best is to have both — a successful career and motherhood."

Diana noticed the concerned look on her face.

"Anyway, I think that what *you* do is far more important than having a child. Any woman could have one, but very few can be as good a doctor as you are."

Andra's eyes, usually expressing determination, had a sad depth now. She was thinking about her daily efforts on behalf of so many mothers and so many babies and felt she had only one wish: to be just a woman that is, a mother.

When she left, she realized that three hours had passed since she came to see Diana, and that it was already dark. The sky was covered with dark clouds and a cold wind was blowing freely through the city. The streets were empty. Just a few rushing passers-by, on their way home, would pop up at some corner and then disappear into dark yards or behind wrought-iron doors.

The wind slowed down, and all of a sudden it grew stiffling hot. Andra looked at the sky. The air was heavy and hazy, and the clouds seemed ready to burst. She set off in a hurry and soon arrived at the main road, joining the crowd at the bus stop. The first rain drops fell. Then, the flow hit the sidewalk, still hot after a day of sunshine. Sparkles of lightning shot across the black sky. The passers-by were running toward shelters. Andra found a spot under a roof edge. This is just a short, spring however, she thought, it won't last. The sidewalk mirrored the street lights, and, people were waiting patiently for the rain to stop.

In no more than fifteen minutes the drops grew scarce. The bus finally arrived. Andra felt cold; she had a strange, upsetting premonition. She got home; her clothes were wet and her hair was unkempt, falling down her back and over her forehead.

She intended to take a shower and go to sleep. She unlocked the door, left he purse and her shoes in the foyer and made for the bedroom. She took off her suit and put on a gown. While she was opening the closet door, she heard a strange noise. For a second, she stood motionless. It was quiet. Then the strange noise made itself heard again. She made for the spot it was coming from, on her tiptoes. She stood for a moment, listening to the sounds coming from the other room, and she heard it again. She opened the door, sharply. On the couch, there was a baby. He was hugging a large white bunny, with green eyes and a big red ribbon on its neck, which Andra kept on the couch. She looked at him, astonished, then checked the apartment to see if anybody else was there. There was no one. She approached the child, took his little hand, looked him in the eyes and said, as if to herself.

"What's the matter with you, bou?"

The baby bent his head back, looking at Andra, and answered in a high, quiet voice:

"I'm playing."

Andra let herself down on the couch, astonished.

"You can talk?"

"Sure."

"How did you get here, who brought you?"

"I came all by myself."

"Where from?"

"From your hospital."

"And what's your name?"

"Robert."

Andra picked up the phone. She asked the delivery ward. She knew she had a new baby by the name of Robert. He was a few days old. A nurse took the call.

"Check the babies. Check on the one called Robert." said Andra.

She waited for a few minutes, then she called in a loud voice:

"Is he there?" and she looked at the couch.

She was alone in the room. The phone fell from her hand; she made from the couch and sat down. She took the green-eyed bunny in her lap and started stroking it. She was thinking that she just had a hallucination; she took her pulse, which was somewhat too fast. She took the thermometer and placed it in her armpit. She lay down on the couch, on her back, thinking that she was all alone. She felt warm, and quiet, and sleepy. She fell asleep.

She woke up late, in the dark; someone had called her name. She thought she had been dreaming. She turned on the light and looked at the thermometer — 103°. She realized she must have caught a cold. Again, she heard her name. She rose from the chair and rushed to the other room. On her bed, wearing her pajama top, was Robert.

"Take me in your arms," he said suppliantly, reaching for her.

"Here you are again?" she said, without really waiting for a response.

She came closer and took him in her arms.

"Who are you?" she asked.

The child tried to hug her, but he couldn't. He just leaned his head on her breast, waiting a few moments and said in a low voice:

"I'm your son."

Andra said nothing. She took the child to the other room and made him a bed on the couch. She returned to the bedroom and sat on her bed for a long time, unable to sleep.

Only much later, when no noise was to be heard from the neighboring apartments and the lights in the windows went off, Andra switched off her own light and went to sleep.

In the morning, her first thought was to go to the other room to see Robert. She opened the door, slowly, so as not to wake him. She looked at the couch. No child. No bedsheet or blanket either, although she remembered having put them on the couch. It was rather late, so she got dressed and left for the hospital. All the way, she kept thinking about what happened the evening before. As soon as she arrived at the hospital she took off her suit, put on the white smock and went to the newborn clinic. She took a look at each other of the babies; she saw Robert lying in his bed: lively, robust, handsome; this was the child whom she had seen the previous evening.

"You came back?" she asked.

Robert looked at her and smiled as a very new baby would smile; then he closed his eyes and went to sleep.

That day, Andra returned again and again to see the newborns. She was watching Robert, she talked to him; she was waiting for his answer, but he didn't seem to understand more than any other infant of his age.

At two o'clock Andra changed her clothes and went home. As she got there, she took her key out of her purse and opened the door, and wondering why she was so careful not to make any noise.

"You're home, ma?" she heard a child's voice.

Andra ran to the room from which the voice was coming. Robert was lying on the couch. He was hugging the white fur bunny with green glass eyes and red ribbon on its neck, the bunny Andra was keeping on her bed. As he saw her, he dropped the toy, extended his arms toward her and said:

"You're late today?"

GREY EYES

Don't you remember? It was raining — the sort of rain that made the night seem even lovelier. Brighter. The sidewalk reflected the carnival-like outfits and the ladies' jewelry. The midnight revelry had taken on an especially jubilant, unrestricted quality. Everyone seemed to be living it up during those first few minutes of the new year. After the crowds counted off the final seconds the horns blew, people began kissing one another. Everyone was carrying a smile, wishing these moments could last for the whole year. The street, as happy as the people, rejected weariness and sleep.

Everything seemed new. The dress I was wearing, the shoes which carried me through the old and new dances. The tie you had spent so much time fixing in front of the mirror. The dreams — they were new as well, sharper, bolder, closer to fulfillment. I was thinking about the past. Not some remote memory, but the immediate past. A past so close, so present. A past which was still holding my arm and following my dreams. I was happy. At least I thought I was. The song sung by a group of youths dressed in lively costumes, the boy running to catch a cab, the kisses exchanged by a girl in a rabbit coat and a young man holding his hat in his left hand. Everything looked warm and conveyed, with more or less certainty, a sense of happiness.

"You're tired. Let's get a cab."

How could I say no? A cab, that would be nice. Warm, pleasant, and fast. We were just a few minutes from home. And then, too, weren't you nice to care about me so much? But this was New Year's Eve. Cabs were scarce. We tried to get one, but after a few attempts with cabs hurriedly claimed by other people, all we got was frustration.

"You want a cab?" asked a kid carrying flowers tied over a long stick, according to the local custom. "Just wait, I'll get you one."

That was nice. He was running between the upcoming cars. "Here you are." The door of a blue VW opened, and the driver invited us in. We hesitated for a moment, looked at each other, and then at the driver.

"Get in. I'll take you home."

We did. I told him the name of the neighborhood. The radio was on — at full volume. The music was impregnated with that hot disco stuff. The driver looked quiet. He was about thirty, dressed in a plain grey coat, the kind one might wear to work. He looked tall and skinny. His chestnut hair was closely cropped. At one point he stopped next to a coffee shop, left for a moment, and came back with a pack of cigarettes. He didn't say a word until we got home.

"How much?"

"Just a 'thank you,' that's all. This whole night I have been happy taking home couples in love."

I noticed he looked sad. He had lovely eyes: grey eyes. They were a rare shade. I meant to ask him: "Why are you so sad?" But he stepped on the gas and was gone.

DIALOGUE

I am setting off for a trip underground. I want to find the golden diamond. That's right, a gold-clad diamond. An old man told me that it's hidden in an exploratory mine. Deep underground. Whoever finds it will never feel pain again.

I took along whatever I owned. My thoughts. Eyeglasses. My will. And a bag with food. I haven't forgotten the armour to be put on in case of warning: "Watch out for falling rocks!" I made my appearance at the Gate of Earth. I knocked. What an echo! An automatic system opens the gate. It's large and heavy, made of solid metal. It squeaks horribly. I'm not afraid. My diamond — I must get it. In front of me there's a road. Its end is lost somewhere in the dark. A new road. I am to discover the life inside Terra. Couldn't I be a Columbus? I set off. Up above me, the earth vault looms high. On each side, placed at random, are tiny torches, lit up, spreading light. A mild wind moves the flame. On the walls are strangely shaped shadows. I have my thoughts with me. I open the science drawer. The matter chapter. The shadows go on with their play. I skim, in a hurry, to the chapter about matter and existence. I approach the smooth surface of the wall. I set my hand on a shadow. Nothing happens. I withdraw. I project my hand onto the wall. It is big, strong. I keep walking. I've got the courage. The lights stay behind. In front of me, a black hole opens. I light up my lantern. The walls are moist. Here and there, I see water trickling down. I walk slowly. I listen to the sound of water. Right and left. I notice small galleries. They are leading somewhere. I don't know where. I don't fit in. I can't get through. If I should meet someone, I could ask about the location of the diamond. This road — it's got to have an end. It can't be endless. Human mind cannot grasp endlessness. What if the gallery will go on forever? It would be the end of my life here. In the darkness. Not being able to tell anyone what ails me. No. Everything's got to have an end.

Doesn't human life? The point is — to be able to postpone it. To live as long and as intense as possible. And immortality? Some people work hard to be able to leave something behind. And thus, they live forever. Or do they? This is just a way of talking. Actually, they die too. We all die. But perhaps it's not for nothing. Life does have meaning. I will find the gold-clad diamond, and I shall feel no pain, ever. I'll share it with everyone. Nobody will ever suffer again. Then, I'll be able to accomplish immortal deeds. But what if I die before I find the diamond? I have heard from old people that whoever wishes, with his whole soul, to accomplish something before he dies, close his eyes before he succeeds. Is that true? And why not? Isn't a man's will powerful enough? Couldn't it delay death? Or destroy it?"

"N-n-n-o! Who tries to choke me?"

"It's me."

"You attack from behind, you, scoundrel!"

The bat takes off its claws.

"Who are you?"

"A man."

"What are you looking for?"

"Not for you."

"Talk nicely. I'm weak, when I'm alone, but you know how many of us there are."

I lift the lantern. Lots and lots of bats. Horrible. But I keep my courage.

"I do talk nicely. But not to those who attack from the back."

"It's only natural. I got you because of your hair. Otherwise, I can't see."

"If you had squeezed a little harder I'd have gotten dizzy."

The bats surround me. They are many; they are black. I never cared for mice and bats.

"I'm looking for the golden diamond. Don't you know where it is?"

"It's far, very far away. If we had it, the darkness couldn't crush us. We could live."

"I thought suffering exists only on earth. I want that diamond to destroy human pain."

"Don't you know that people themselves create suffering? You'd better fight the evil on earth. Don't waste your time looking for the diamond."

"I shall go now. Stay well."

"Farewell. We thought you had come with evil thoughts. Take care of yourself."

I left. What do the bats know about people? They can't see; they have no eyes.

The road is too dark. I lift my lantern. The walls grow damp. The bats are far behind me. I'm alone. I look at my watch. It works. It's daytime. What a day! Dark, cold, wet. It must be sunny on the earth. I feel tired. I sit down on my back-pack. I'm dozing. I don't know for how long. I hear noises. I give a start. It's dark. I light up the lantern. There are shadows on a wall. They move. I don't see anything. I keep looking. I'm dizzy. Maybe I'm not quite awake. I wipe my forehead with water I collect from a wall. I feel better. I approach the shadows. Down on the ground I see worms. The shadows are theirs. They have made a circle. Two of them are in the middle. I think, they're fighting. They scream. Something had happened. They coil around each other. They throw themselves about. They crush each other. The others are watching. They don't interfere. Those in the middle, they're killing each other. I try to separate them. "None of your business!" one of them yells — I give up. The fight has stopped. Both are weary. They move toward a tiny pool of water. They calm down. Then they face each other. Now I know, they are female worms.

"I haven't come to fight with you. I want an explanation. Why don't you leave my man alone?"

"You've got no evidence against me," the other said. She rubbed, coquettishly, her so-called head against the ground. "Your husband is cheating on you. Leave him. Give him up."

"I care for him. You give up."

"Perhaps, he betrays you every day with someone else."

"Could be. They'll give up, all of them."

"What if he doesn't give up?"

"Don't you think he won't?"

"I'm positive."

She has a desperate look. She coils, sighs, and she leaves, moving heavily. The surrounding worms make room for her to pass. She moves faster and faster. Nobody watches her — only me. It's easy, I don't even have to move. She moves towards a pool — a couple of inches wide. She lingers a moment on the side, coils, stretches, and throws herself into the water. She's drowning. I dip my finger in and save her.

"What for? It's not worth it."

"You mind people. Don't interfere with those you can't comprehend. Let me go."

"I don't want to die."

She doesn't answer. She coils about my finger. She touches her head with her tail. Then she relaxes and falls down. I look at her. She's dead. She has killed herself. I take her and put her in the middle of the circle. The others keep talking. Then they notice. They are silent. A worm crawls up, quickly, with a scream. All the others make room for him. I leave.

Where could that diamond be? I turn off the lantern. I must use it sparingly. It's dark. Tomb-dark. I keep walking, inertly. I can't step to the right or to the left. I have no choice. Now and then, I see small outlets to the outside. They are too narrow for me. Too narrow for people. I was told that the diamond is to be found on the people's road. I hit something. I give a start. It's soft and cold. I turn on the lantern. It's horrible. In front of me I see a shapeless bulk of matter. It's moving. It's dark and shiny and greasy. It moves heavily. Two grey balls are staring at me. They are rolling feverishly. They stop and fix upon me. I try to go back.

"Don't be frightened."

"Who are you?"

"You see who I am. I don't know any more about myself. Just that I'm strong and large."

"Are there many of the likes of you around here?"

"I'm alone."

"How come?"

"They're dead, all of them. I'm the only one left."

"What do you do?"

"Nothing."

"Do you want to help me?'

"I never did a thing like that. In fact, I have never done anything. I could try."

"I want to find the gold-clad diamond."

"Nobody knows where it is, because nobody has gotten to the end of the road."

"Do you want to come along?"

"Not now. Later. I'm hungry."

"I could feed you."

"I eat only live flesh."

"Do you kill?"

"Why not? One must live."

"I can't otherwise."

I sit next to him. Do I need such a companion? Can I fall back now? I decide to go on. We set off together. He leads me. He crawls. I hear him. I follow him. I'm tired. The animal is strong. I want to stop him.

"I'm hungry," he says.

He doesn't stop. My food doesn't please him. He moves on fast. I follow him. I'm freezing. The earth is wet. I slip, I fall, I rise. I fall behind. I switch on the light. I run, I catch up with him. He has stopped. He's waiting for me.

"Let's move," I say.

"Shut up. Wait."

He's on the watch. I look ahead to some creature in white fur.

"Don't. Don't kill it." I scream.

"Turn off the light."

I don't. He looks at me. His eye balls keep rolling fast. He rises. He's bigger than I thought. He's bigger than I am. I stay silent. I turn off the light. He springs. I hear a scream. I remain where I am. It's quiet. I turn on the light. I see him. He's eating. He has blood all over him. My heart sinks. I shouldn't have. This beast scares me.

"What's your name?"

"I haven't any."

He's bolting. He laughs. He's happy. He takes the victim's head into his small, thick paws. Two red eyes are staring at him. I come closer. The red eyes are staring at me.

"How many have you killed?"

He laughs. He laughs at me.

"How do I know. Thousands and thousands. Now I can't walk anymore. I need a rest." He ponders, then he talks again. "And come to think of it, why should I do you favors? Maybe you're tastier than this fur."

"You're kidding."

He stays silent. I put on my brick outfit. I'm protected. This way, I'm not tasty. I pass him by. The road starts climbing. I see a huge rock. Should I throw it at him? I don't think twice. There's no time. He's falling asleep. I try the rock. It's not heavy to remove. I push it towards the beast. It gets him! The beast roars. I turn on the light. The rock squashes him. But it has cut off the way back. Never mind. I'm determined to move on. The lantern dies out. I turn it around. I try to switch the knob. It doesn't work. Someone's laughing. I'm frightened. The echo fills the underground. I want to advance. I hit a wall. Behind me is the rock. To the right and left are walls. The laughter shakes them. I throw myself about. The brick outfit melts. The water runs down my back. I try again to get out. Walls are about me. I fret uselessly. I stop. I put on my glasses. They slip down and break. I look for my backpack. Gone. I try thinking. I feel depressed. The laughter reverberates in my ears. I see nothing. It's dark. Pitch-dark. I want to return to the earth. However . . . something glitters. The gold-clad diamond. Here it is. I want to seize it. It disappears. The laughter, again. I tremble. I don't move. I feel something next to me. Something touches me. Or does it? I must find the diamond. I've come all the way here. I can't leave without it. I see it. I reach for it. It disappears. I feel a cold wind. No. Someone's running around me. Someone cold touches my face. I want to catch him. I can't. I feel my clothes. They are torn. I touch my hair. I'm dizzy. My hair is falling out. I feel no pain. I feel my face again. It's me, I'm alive. My heart is beating. Someone watches me. He laughs. Again. I'm strong, I must resist. I lean on a wall. I shall wait. The wall quakes. I step aside. I see weak lights. They are moving. I see huge jaws, grimacing. Fire tongues. Eyes. They're running around. A green skeleton steps in front of me. It stays a while, then disappears. Skulls. The teeth are phosphorescent. A huge tongue comes close. It touches me. It's cold. It's rough. I'm scared. I can't move. If I only could get out. Eyes popped out of their sockets. They are red. Something pulls my hand. I look. A hairy monster. It has big ears. It disappears. Shadows play on the wall. More skulls.

It's quiet. I stay for a few seconds. In front of me, something floats. I can see. It's an infant in swaddling clothes. It's stopped. It has the face of an old man. All wrinkled. Deeply. The mouth is torn. I touch his face. Rigid. His eyes are moving, like two black holes. He tries laughing. His mouth twists. Beyond the lips, there's a hole. I close my eyes. I try to find a solution. I can't. I must wait. I open my eyes. It's dark: I can't see anything any longer. Shadows appear on the wall. I scarcely perceive them. They've disappeared. The ugliness repulses me. I'm afraid I can't go back. I wait. It's quiet and still. I can finally see the phosphorescent needles of my watch. It's night on earth, as well. For a long time, nothing has happened. Nothing bothers me. I look at my watch again. I've been here for two hours. The quiet is cold. Chilly. I sit down on the ground.

I hear a command: "Get up." A thick, strong voice. A determined one.

I get up. I'm next to a wall. In front of me, I see a skeleton. It disappears. Two people appear on the same spot. They are thin, with corpse-livid faces. One of them has a scar across his belly. His eyes come out of their sockets. They approach me. They move around. They're watching me. They've left two holes behind them. They go back. They sit at their master's feet. Two more people appear. They are skinny and tall, with fixed gazes. They move heavily in search of a free spot. Their joints quiver. The cave fills up. Now and then a pair of eyes come to look at me. None of the newcomers touches me. They say nothing. They stand in place. They don't breathe. Once in a while, one of them twists his face, with difficulty. They are skinny. All of them are skinny. And pale, translucent. Under their skin, one can see the bones. The faces have various expressions, but all are sad. They communicate without talking, which I realize from the movement of their eyes. They people in the middle step apart. Between them, I see the diamond. I want to come closer. Something cold sticks to my chest. It stops me.

"You can't get anything without giving," a voice says. I don't know who said that. Nobody moved.

"What should I give?" I hardly can utter.

I have no strength left. I'm weak. I'm weary.

"We got it in exchange for our lives."

I close my eyes. I'm thinking of the earth. Of the sun. Of people. Of life. I gain strength.

"No," I shout, "never!"

I hear the laughter again. The diamond falls. It's on the ground. It's shining. Above it stronger and larger than everything, there is a skull. Arrows of fire dart out of his eye-sockets. His teeth unclench.

"My laws rule here. You have killed."

Next to me I see the frightful monster I killed.

"I killed to defend myself."

"You didn't have to," says the white fur with red eyes.

Everyone disappears. Only shadows, hardly perceivable, remain. In front of me, I still see the large skull.

"Give me the diamond," I say.

"You can only have the diamond here."

"I want it on earth. To do away with pain."

"People have their own laws. Whoever wants to do away with pain, let him come here."

"Then, I shall go back. Without your diamond."

He laughs. Again. Long, long laughter. This laughter irritates me, frightens me.

"You must pay. You have killed. Here."

He laughs. Everywhere. About me, there's a pool of blood. I spring to my feet, involuntarily. I fall again. I slip. I can't keep still. Death turns me over and out.

"I'll pay nothing," I say.

Death pulls me up. Up above the ground. He pushes me to my feet, with a shock. It hurts. I stand up. I close my eyes. I get to pull my thoughts together. I remember earth. I'm looking for a way to get out of here. The old people say those who wish with their whole heart to accomplish something before they die cannot die before seeing their dream come true. I want my dream to come true. I want to do away with pain. I repeat that in my mind. Over and over. I'm not listening to what Death is saying. I don't see him anymore. I am strong.

I hear a voice at the back of my head. It whispers.

"Don't you know the people create pain for themselves? Don't look for the diamond — it's useless."

It's the bat. I want to catch it. It disappears.

Death is still here.

"I shall pay — only after I've committed evil," I say aloud. Death gets mad. Its bones unbind. Around him, fire arrows dance. I throw myself on the rock barring the way back. I'm strong, I push it aside, I try. It's heavy. I keep struggling. I must. It moves. Death watches me. The rock falls back. I move it again. I'm sweating. I'm hot. Good. Anyway, it's freezing here. The wall moves. It quakes. That's how walls fall, I think. The rock collapses. The road is open. I must get back to the earth I keep telling myself. I'm not afraid. Now I know everything. I must live. My dream must come true. I'll make it come true. I'll find the root of evil. I'm strong. I'm a human being. I walk fast. I run. I run all the way. I don't look back. I reach the iron gate. It doesn't open. I knock. No use. I look at it. It cannot be stronger than I am. People make thousands and thousands of gates, I think. A rock falls down next to me. I haven't got my brick outfit any longer. Nor food. I've forgotten all about food. Now I'm hungry. I'm hungry. I haven't got anything now. Only my thoughts and my will. I see a worm.

"I want to help you. I am. . ."

"I know who you are. She killed herself because of you. You're too small to help me."

The worm stays quiet. He watches me.

"Anything small can grow large."

He's wise. I'm sorry to have insulted him. I shan't do it again. He's not hurt. He wants to help me. He crawls up the gate. He's right in the middle. He penetrates the notch between the two halves. He stays there for a long time. Then he comes out.

"Now push. Harder, go on, push."

I push. With all my strength. I must open it. I hear a squeak. I see light. The gate opens.

"Thank you, little worm."

He coils around. He smiles. I look back. I'm happy. "Bye now," I shout. I hear laughter again. Then, out of the dark hole, comes a voice.

"You'll come back."

"Maybe," I shout, "later."

SORROW

"Time does fly," thinks Edward. "I feel as if it were the first time I saw snow. Oh yes, it looks like it's my first snow."

He walks slowly, heavily. His shoes sink into the snow. It's evening. The large snowflakes sparkle as he crosses the beam of a street lantern. "One more year is over. One of the many." He remembers how a friend taught him to measure his age according to his heart's age. He feels his heart is heavy with so many years. All of them alike. That's what he thinks. One more year is done. He tries to get to the bottom line. He never tried that before. It is probably a token of maturity: trying to turn one's eyes toward one's self. He knows that he has noble thoughts, and that he can do good things, useful things. He knows, because sometimes he did them. But they were few. He would like them to be many more.

The snow keeps falling. The street is immaculately white. The houses are diamond-clad. With their dimly illuminated windows, they look like fairy-houses. And the match girl should be nearby. But no, there is no child here to cry under somebody's window. He thinks about his son. How is his son going to grow up? He misses the boy. It's too bad. Life must go on. The years go by. His son might have another father now. The boy might think that the real father is the one who takes care of him. How much he hated the foolishness of his youth! Those senseless acts. If only he could start everything anew. He would know how one should live. He would do everything so that his son has his real father next to him. Loneliness is sad.

He heard many times: "I would like to be young, but to keep my present wisdom." He knows exactly what that means, now.

The street is empty. It's only him and the snowflakes. He turns around the corner, and now he is headed down the road which he had once walked, years and years ago.

He hears horses hitting the ground with their shoes, behind him. Horses here, in the city? He turns around, sharply. A black spot against the white snow; it comes closer. Edward slows down and looks. It's a pitch-black hearse, moving slowly. Two horses, black as well, advance through the snow. The hearse is followed by three men, middle-aged, not old, bare-headed in spite of the snowfall. Edward approaches one of them.

"Good evening," he says.

The stranger answers in a low voice, without looking at him.

"Who's in there?" Edward asks.

"Just a man."

"You're taking him to the cemetery?"

"Sure."

"Why at night, at this hour?"

The man who is holding his hat looks at Edward. He looks Edward up and down, lingering on his eyes. They look at each other. They walk next to one another. They are accompanied by the horsehoe beat. The stranger looks down. The snowflakes hit his face.

"I don't know," the stranger finally says.

Edward walks along with the three men. He would like to learn more about the dead man. The stranger next to him looks sad. He might be a relation of the deceased.

Nobody says anything. The hearse moves on, slowly. The four men walk behind. Only the horses' step can be heard.

Edward had seen quite a few deaths in his life. However, he had never shared the sorrow of those who stayed behind. He avoided going to the cemetery. He had been many times in a dissecting room, among scores of bodies. He wasn't afraid of the dead, but he was afraid of abyssmal quiet of the the tombs. He follows the hearse, now, and he doesn't know who he is seeing off to his last shelter.

"Was this a relative of yours?" Edward asks.

The stranger shakes his head.

"A friend?"

"No."

"Did you know him?"

"No."

"Did the others?"

"No. Except for the woman in the hearse."

Edward looks up to the hearse. He perceives the shape of a woman in mourning clothes.

"I've never seen him. As the hearse was passing by, I asked the others, as you asked me. They didn't know anything. They just thought that a man shouldn't be alone, not even on his last way."

He grew silent.

The houses stood behind. The road stretches before them. The horses move with difficulty. The hearse stops. The coachman comes down and take the bridle. The hearse keeps sliding back on soft snow.

"They say, a man gets heavy as he approaches the grave; he doesn't want to be buried. He doesn't want to be left alone," the stranger says.

The horses take off. The snowflakes dance around. The way uphill is difficult. The trees fencing the road seem to follow the mourners.

The four men walk slowly, with their eyes down. Suddenly, a shriek — a cry of despair and hopelessness. Everyone gives a start. The woman takes the dead body in her arms. She holds it close. Perhaps, she sees the entrance to the cemetery. The coachman gives the woman a matchbox. She lets the body go, takes a match and lights up a candle. She bends over the coffin. She lays her face over the dead man's chest. The hearse takes off again. It enters the gate.

It's quiet. Here and there, tiny lights flicker in lanterns. The hearse advances through the main lane, toward the chapel.

Edward has a bitter smile. "Such an idyllic image and such a tragic reality," he thinks. Crosses, short and tall, seem to be the guardians of earth beds. The flowers have been covered by the snow. Edward sees something nearby that seems to be a newly covered tomb. He comes closer, and on the cross, made out of yellow wood, he sees the photograph of a young man. He has a strange feeling: pity and fear. He is afraid of death and of loneliness.

The hearse moves away. He wants to run after it, to catch up with it. He wants to be close to those strangers, to feel them breathing nearby. He is ashamed. He can't run.

They would laugh at him. He takes off, making large steps. He feels heavy, clumsy. He moves down the alley. There are tombs on each side. He doesn't look at them. His legs are carrying him away faster and faster. He looks at the snowflakes. "Still dancing," he thinks, "even here." He thinks that his frenzied dance is senseless. The hearse is no longer in sight. He approaches the chapel. The door is open. Inside, lights are flickering. He perceives the shape of a coffin. He runs to the right and sees the hearse. He slows down. The horses are hitting the ground with their shoes. The men are not there.

He looks around. He notices the men carrying the coffin. He comes closer. There is one more man. It must be the cemetery warden, a sturdy man with a wide beard. Or perhaps, he's the priest. The coffin is on the ground next to the tomb. The woman looks at the body. The newcomer tries to cover the coffin. The woman's cry breaks the silence. One of the strangers holds her arm. The woman doesn't cry any longer. She lights a candle. She protects it from the snow. Her face looks stone-hard. She is pale, skinny. She could be at most forty. The dead man was pretty young, too. Two men fix the coffin lid. The woman is motionless. The candle goes off.

"Won't you have any religious service for him?" asks Edward.

Nobody listens to him. The men arrange two ropes under the coffin. They try to lift it up. Edward gives them a hand, too. The woman steps aside. She leans on a cross. The coffin is let down into the grave. The woman bends over. She pushes the snow aside and sinks her hand into the earth. She takes a handful of earth and slowly lets it fall over the coffin.

The others do the same thing. Edward watches. "Why are they doing this?" he asks himself. The bearded man who arrived last picks up the shovel. Pebbles are thrown over the coffin; muffled noises come from the grave.

The woman signs herself. She bends next to the cross and lights up a lantern. She stays immobile for a while, looking at the grave, which fills, becoming shallower and shallower.

"What does existence mean?" Edward asks himself.

For a few minutes, the men and the woman stand still, rock-still. The warden is done with his job.

"The flowers," the woman gives a start.

She gets up and runs toward the hearse. Everyone's watching her. She comes back slowly, holding a large bunch of white flowers. She arranges them over the tomb. She kneels. Her eyes look into remoteness.

"Let's go," the warden says. "May he rest in peace."

And he signs himself.

The men head toward the hearse. The coachman helps the woman up. She doesn't resist in any way.

"We leave you by yourself now," she says, as if for herself.

"Sometimes, one is all by himself even while alive." The warden says.

"I can give you a ride to the town," says the coachman.

Everyone is stepping over tombs, awhite with snow. Somewhere, behind them, there is a fresh tomb. A black spot over the white plain dotted by crosses. The snow keeps falling. The flakes play the game, sprightly yet sadly. They fall over the tomb. Soon, no one will be able to tell when it had been dug. The flakes are large. Now and then, in their play, they sparkle. Strange sparks, lasting but an instant. Only their play is eternal.

THE STREET

As he usually does in the morning, George opened the window. He leaned his elbows on the window sill, and sunk his face into his palms.

"The kid has got to be sent some place," his mother was saying in the other room. "He's on vacation, he's bored. It is ever hot in this city . . . Don't you see anything strange about him?"

The father went on shaving, watching his face in the mirror.

"Don't you see any change?" the mother insisted.

"No. What's that?"

"He's losing weight."

"He's growing," said the father.

"George, what are you up to over there?" mother called.

"I'm watching the street, Mother," the boy answered quietly. The mother went about her business.

"He's thirteen," she said. Now you should talk to him, tell him more about people, he should know all kinds of things. . ."

"Mother," George called, "I'm going to the movies."

"That early in the morning they don't . . ."

But the apartment door was being slammed.

"Good morning, Miss Ann," George said.

"Good morning, George. Where are you going that early?"

Ann was young — she was about 22; she was a college student.

"I'm going shopping. What about you?"

"I'm going to see my mother."

"Can I ask you something. . ." George murmured.

"Sure, go ahead."

George blushed. How could he confide in her? He decided to lie.

"Can I walk with you?"

"If you wish; however, it's a long walk," Ann said. George felt happy. Quite happy. He wished the walk would last forever. He watched every day at his window, hoping to see her. When he would go to school, he would try to come home as soon as he could. He dropped his friends. Now that he was on vacation he would like to see her more often.

In the bus, George tried to buy a ticket for Ann, but he wasn't fast enough: she paid for herself. George felt offended. "She keeps treating me like a kid," he thought. True, she was slightly taller than he was, but he was growing fast. Besides, what did that matter, as long as he loved her. He was waiting, hour after hour, to see her face. He wanted to look into her dark eyes, to stroke her heavy hair, fastened in a loop; he would like to undo it and kiss it, he would like to touch her hand. That was all. He had to see her every day, every hour.

"How was school this year?" she asked.

"OK," George said, feeling irritated. Couldn't she ask something else? Why doesn't she ask how I'm spending my time now, in summer. Maybe, I'd tell her that I spend it at my window. I could tell her that no way am I going to leave the city, because I want to see her.

"Are you planning to go on vacation any place?" he asked.

"To my grandparents."

"For how long?"

"I would like to stay until the school starts."

George grew pale. Not seeing her for two months? That was impossible. What could he do? Could he tell her? He wouldn't be able to see her if she leaves.

"Miss Ann," he said, stammering, "I must tell you something."

"What is it, George, tell me."

"Please, don't be angry with me, please, I have two tickets to a movie for tomorrow morning. Would you like to come along?"

Ann looked surprised.

"What movie?" she asked.

"It's . . ." George tried to remember every movie which was playing downtown. "Black Tulip," he said, happy about having been able to remember.

"Oh, I would like to see that! It's with Roger Moore, it's well worth seeing."

"Look what she's thinking about," he thinks. "Roger Moore. What about me? Oh well, the main thing is she accepted. I must run and get the tickets."

They arrived at her mother's.

"So, I'll see you tomorrow at 10," he said. "I'll be waiting for you at the window."

"Fine" she said. "See you tomorrow." She gave him her hand and he took it with excitement.

The next thing George did was to run back home to get some money from his mother. Then he went to get the tickets.

The next day, everything went better than he ever expected. She came, in spite of his doubts. The seats were good. During the movie, George watched her, without her noticing. She was all taken by the movie. When the hero was escaping from the jail, she was so excited she took George's hand and held it for a while. George forgot about the movie. He held his hand out, breathless, experiencing one of the loveliest moments of his life.

"Oh, I'm sorry," she said when she realized that she was still holding his hand. The movie was over. She sensed what was going on in George's heart and decided to be careful from then on.

As they were leaving the theater she took out her purse and asked about the ticket price.

"It's nothing," he said. "I wanted to sit next to you for two hours — I wish I could do it every day."

"That's nice," she said, as if she thought that was a joke, "but it's just impossible. And what about your vacation? Aren't you going any place?"

I'll go; that's what Mom says."

"Well, you better listen to her."

"Sure," said George, resenting her talking this way. He felt she knew what this was all about. He felt ashamed. He wanted to go home at once. They had hardly reached the corner when he said:

"I must excuse myself now. I have to see a friend. It's better for you not to be seen with me."

Ann had no time to express her surprise: he disappeared. The girl shrugged her shoulders and went home.

George made a detour and went home as well.

The next day, he opened the window as usual. He stood behind the curtains. He wanted to see her again. However, she stayed at home the whole day. He took a chair, pushed it next to the window, sat down and tried to read. In the evening he let the book fall. He saw Ann coming out of the building. She was carrying a suitcase. His heart sunk.

"What are you doing, George?" Mother asked.

"I'm watching the street."

THE WANDERER

Victor took the child's hand. The Boy raised his eyes toward him and smiled. He had big, green eyes. The two of them set off each other. The street was deserted. The rain has eased off only a few minutes before and the sidewalk was still wet. The trees were spreading their fragrance in the air, trying their strength as it were, against the aroma of the backyard flowers. Once in a while, the child would raise his head, gaze into Victor's eyes, and as soon as he was sure that Victor was looking at him, he would smile a most uninhibited smile.

It was getting darker and darker, and night was coming, along with cool air.

"I'm cold," said the boy.

Victor stopped. He took off his coat and put it around the child's shoulders. The boy put it on. He turned up the sleeves, which were too long for him, and again extended a small hand toward Victor.

"Are you cold?" Victor asked.

The boy shook his head. The coat covered his shorts and he looked like someone dressed in charity gifts. Victor smiled, for the boy's face was so serious, and his clothes so funny.

"Very becoming," he said.

"Sure!" the boy said quite seriously. When I grow up, I'm going to buy myself a suit just like yours. When I was your age I used to wear a long coat and a top hat. Guess it was about two hundred years ago. This was the last time. . ."

"When you were my age?!"

"You heard me"

Victor threw a surreptitious look at the child. Then he asked him all kinds of questions, to hear him talk. He noticed that the boy had a voice too harsh for his age, that his speech was correct, and his reasoning was that of a grown-up. He stopped. Then, he drew the child toward him, kneeling in order that he could have him closer and asked:

"What's your name?"

"Victor," said the child.

"How come, Victor? Victor is my name, too."

"That's good. So what? Victor was my name in every life."

Victor was thinking that the boy must be a dreamer. He must have heard all kinds of talk in his family, and now he was making up things. They say all children lie. Not that they were fond of lying; they were just wishful thinkers, that's all.

"How old are you?"

"Thousands of years old."

"You're a funny little fellow! At your age, you should show more respect."

"I will, but I'm still thousands of years old."

"This is going too far," Victor thought, "I should take him home fast."

"You say you live on Hope Street?"

"I might have said so. Who knows?!"

"How did you get lost?"

"Lost by whom?"

"What do you mean, by whom? By your parents."

"What parents?"

"Look, I like you, but don't try to be funny. Come on, let's move faster!"

They were walking side by side, silently. The boy poked his hands into the coat sleeves. Now and then, he would stay behind, and then he would have to run to catch up with Victor.

When they passed the Hope Street corner it was really dark.

"I've already seen this house at some time," said the child, pointing at a white colonial with lighted windows.

Victor seized his hand nervously and walked toward the house. He rang the bell. A man came out, blond-haired, blue-eyed, with a warm, peaceful gaze; a man of average height.

"Is this your son?" Victor asked.

The blond-haired man shook his head.

"No," he said. "Unfortunately I have no children. "Whose son are you, big fellow?" he asked the boy.

The boy squeezed his lips. He said nothing.

The blond-haired man took his hand and drew him closer.

"If you want," the child said looking straight into his eyes, "if you want, I can be yours."

"I would like you to be mine, but your parents would be mad."

The child looked at Victor. He noticed his sad, ashy eyes. Then he left the blond-haired man and turned back to Victor. He seized his clothes and curled himself up next to Victor.

"Then, he's not yours?" Victor asked the blond man.

"No. I don't think I ever saw him."

The two of them left. They walked a few steps down the Hope Street, then they stopped.

"Which way?" Victor asked.

"To your place," said the boy.

"What do you mean, my place? Why should I take you? Tell me, where do you live? Tell me where, or else I will just leave you on the street. do you hear?"

Victor sank into thoughts. He wasn't used to unusual situations and had no idea what to do. Some story — this kid running into him. What was the way out? Victor found the boy in the park which he walked through daily on his way home. The kid just stuck to Victor; he was crying and saying he was lost. At this point there was no way to get rid of him.

Now it was really dark. Black clouds were obstructing the sky. The man and the boy were standing in the middle of the road facing each other.

"Which way?" Victor asked again

He got no answer.

The boy leaned on a fence. "Look how people run away from luck!" he was thinking. He looked at the sky. The raindrops were starting to fall.

"I'll give you back your coat and you go home," said the boy.

"How about you?"

"I'll stay here. I shall die now, and I shall come alive again, who knows when. I die whenever I'm not loved. People must stop and love me again and again."

Victor blushed.

"Are you starting all over? Shut up, I tell you. Come here."

The rain began to fall. The child approached Victor.

"I'm your good fortune, your lucky moment which you're ready to let go. Take me along."

"My good fortune!"

"You understand nothing! Pity! It's so good when people think a lot! I don't mean to offend you, however, people do have that chance; they can think."

Victor wasn't listening anymore. The rain was growing heavier. He put his coat over the child's head and they set off. "I'm going to take him to my place. Tomorrow I'm going to look for his folks. Maybe, after he sleeps he'll talk normally."

They rambled through a few streets. The rain kept falling. Victor was thinking about the boy's fate. "A poor boy, abandoned or lost. However, someone may be crying for having lost him. I'm going to call the police, the newspapers, who knows, maybe one day his parents will come for him. The kid looks sick. He might even have a fever."

He stopped. Suddenly, he had a strange feeling. He couldn't hear the boy's steps anymore. He really couldn't. He looked back. The kid wasn't there, he had disappeared. A few feet behind him he saw his coat hanging on a fence. Victor took the coat and put it on. He looked over the fence and into the yard but couldn't see anybody. He heard no noise but the even beating of the rain drops on the pavement. He started looking in all the yards. He ran up the street. Then he called:

"Victor, hey, little Victor, where are you?"

The clouds were still over the town. Victor kept running through the streets. Exhausted, he stopped on a corner. He looked at his watch. It was midnight. He returned to Hope Street. The lights in the white house were turned off. He saw no passers-by whom he could ask about the boy. He decided to go home. He was feeling sad and sorry for not having taken care of the boy. Perhaps, he shouldn't have scolded him, shouldn't have yelled.

He came to a taxi station and waited for a few minutes before a car was available. On his way he looked out of the taxi, right and left, hoping to see the boy, but there was no one on the streets. He arrived home. Once more, he looked back, then opened the gate. He took the key and put it into the lock. The rain hadn't stopped.

Victor felt a breath of air on his cheek. Again, he had a strange feeling. He looked back. In the shadow of the roof he saw a child's shape. He approached it. It was the green-eyed boy.

"What are you doing here?"

"I just came. Otherwise, you'd have walked me through the streets all night. If you don't want me, I'll go and you will never see me in your life, but you'll always wish I were with you."

"How did you know the house?"

"I've known it for decades."

"But you've never been here."

"I used to live around here, a long time ago."

Victor opened the door. He smiled at the boy and took his hand. They entered the house. Outside, the rain kept falling.

THE PLANTS

George was sitting on a chair facing the desk. He was leaning his elbow on a tiny table intended for visitors. A few files were laying on the desk, which was large and adorned with carvings. On one file cover one could see the inscription: "to clear up." Next to that were a few sheets of paper looking like applications. A white marble inkpot was probably ornamental, for next to it lay a long ballpoint pen and in the middle of the open file, in front of the large, carved chair facing the desk, there was a Montblanc fountain pen in its white box.

The dark man, handsome, in spite of his grey hair, short, wearing a latest-style dark suit, was holding the piece of paper George had brought. The man read it, but he didn't say a thing; he was considering it as if it were a difficult philosophical excerpt. On the wall, there were photographs of the man who was sitting on the carved chair in his blue suit. In the same office, next to the window, on the table protected by a sturdy glass plate there was a colored crystal goblet. Beneath the glass plate, there were all kinds of photographs of the dark man, and of other people, perhaps friends or acquaintances. Between the two tables, closer to the wall, there was a plant with large, dented leaves.

"If there's no way, there's no way" said George, having lost his patience, but apparently quite calm.

"You see, my friend," the dark man started, "it certainly isn't that difficult, but the timing is wrong. Had you come earlier. . ."

"You told me to come now," George answered. "It's all right. I'm sure, if you hadn't known me before, if we hadn't been friends once, everything would be different. As a matter of fact, what is it I'm asking, if not to make something good, to state a truth?"

This way of thinking didn't suit the dark man. He didn't like anyone to remind him about a past friendship. Bygones should be bygones. Today he had other friends. Once, they had been on a first-name basis, but now, even if he called his visitor George he expected to be addressed as Mr. so-and-so. It was proper for George to show more respect, and not to remind him about truth, because he knew himself what the truth was, and anyway, George shouldn't have made this request. He could have gone to anyone else. The dark man had to get rid of him, if possible, in such a way as to prevent George from spoiling his image afterwards. Suppose he promises, what was there to lose? Except that George wasn't happy with words. He knew a lot about promises.

The dark man rose from his chair, turned about the desk, and sat down on the chair next to the small table. He started telling George something which sounded like a promise, but George couldn't hear his words. He was thinking about his friend and colleague asking his advice. He also remembered those sad days when his friend had no job and needed help. Now, he was so different! His speech was cautious and aloof; he spoke coldly, and each of his words was self-assured. He was delighted with himself and once in a while, was sticking his pipe into the corner of his mouth.

George rose and thanked him, without knowing himself for what, then he made for the door, having taken his paper from the table. At this point the secretary called, and the dark man asked someone in. A short man entered; he was round-faced, had an extensive bald spot, blond hair, and was somewhat plump. The newcomer noticed George; he knew George, but he walked toward the host, smiling, and extended his hand. George knew that they hated each other to death. He left them: he opened the door noiselessly and stepped into the secretary's office. He looked at his watch: it was five. He had wasted his time for nothing. How come he hadn't foreseen the result? He told himself it was embarrassing even to think that such a man had been his friend. Birds of a feather. . .

But this man and George — how different they were. The strangest thing was, George thought, that the man used to be such a candid, easily elated soul. That was quite a while ago. They both grew older, but George was still keeping a share of ingenuity. He had heard once that not everyone held out on the way up. That in some people, the humaneness was killed by the chair they were filling. George wouldn't believe it. To him, life's watchword was: frankness and truth. He was trying to comfort himself. "One instance doesn't mean habit, routine. However, why should there be that instance? The evil had to be eradicated," he thought and he felt his belief in man was shaken. He felt afraid, and his wish for justice to come through was filling his mind with haunting words.

He was on the point of lighting a cigarette when he heard screams from the neighboring room. The secretary rushed in. She sprung out at once, terrified. Then, she beckoned George to go in and called out for scissors. She left and came back in a minute, carrying a small knife.

George forgot his reflections. He knew for sure that the Good will overcome, and that the Evil's worst enemy was conscience alone. What was happening now was strange, and he felt overcome with fear. The plant had extended its stem and leaves, rolled around the men, and it couldn't be loosened anymore. He had to rescue the two bodies struggling power-lessly. He tried to loosen the plant, coiled up around them. The girl tried to cut it, but the plant surrounded her as well. Now the plant made for George. He stumbled over a large vase standing in the corner of the corridor and broke it. He took a fragment and threw it at the plant. The plant was wound up to the ceiling now, as if it were looking for a victim, it was rolling downstairs.

George ran. The doorman saw him and with his eyes wide open in surprise tried to catch him, believing he was a thief. But George reached the street, closed the heavy door, and nobody followed him. Now, he was walking slowly, tired as if after a fight, wiping the sweat from his face. People were passing him by, some of them serene, others worried, happy or sad. George stopped in front of a garden and looked at the flowers, brightly colored and breathing the joy of life. A gentle breeze touched the flowers and made George shiver. He looked at his watch. It was 6 o'clock, precisely the time when he was supposed to meet Ann. He jumped on a bus and got off to downtown. She was waiting for him, although he was twenty minutes late. He kissed her on the cheek, as usual, and took her arm.

They were walking in silence. After a while, Ann broke in:

"Are you upset?"

"No," George said, although the sadness of his outlook was obvious.

They say frank people cannot hide their thoughts and feelings. George was like that. And Ann knew him well.

"You're lying," Ann said, without being nasty; then she thought George was trying to keep something from her and grew sad at once.

"What do you know about lying?" George asked.

The girl gave him a worried look. Now she was sure that something unpleasant had happened to him.

They were walking arm in arm. For quite a while they said nothing.

The next day George had a new idea: Ann had to move in. His parents wouldn't object. He had to talk to her. After all that had happened, he was afraid to leave her alone. He and his parents lived in a suburb. After work, George took the bus to Ann's house. He found her tidying up. She was surprised to see him. It would have been easy for him to pick up a phone and tell her he was coming. George sat on the couch. Ann kept on vacuuming. The noise was aggravating.

"How come you don't ask me why I'm here?" said George loudly.

"Wait until I'm done, then we can talk. I hope it's not that urgent."

George said nothing. He was looking around, and every item looked familiar. He had been a frequent visitor. The girl turned off the vacuum cleaner. The house became silent. She detached the hose, which rolled up her hand. George rose swiftly. He imagined the hose extending and coiling up about both of them. The girl looked at him fearfully. She asked nothing and he told her he just wanted to help her put the vacuum cleaner away. He seized the hose, which filled him with unexpected fear. He rolled it carefully as if it could break. Ann noticed that, took the hose from him, rolled it energetically and put it away in a cardboard box. George was watching, and all he saw was a red pipe with grooves and swellings, like a huge worm.

When the girl was finished, George drew her next to him on the couch. For a moment, he forgot the climbing plant, for Ann was close. He felt in her, alive, the spirit of womanhood in all its wholesomeness: she was impish and warm, whimsical and tender, demure and earnest. She was more down-to-earth than he, although she was impossibly superstitious and fearful. He was blaming himself for not having made up his mind about their getting married. One thing was certain: they had to be together, they both wanted that.

"I want you to move in with us," George said abruptly.

The girl seemed puzzled. She didn't know what he meant. Did he want them to get married? She had a place to live in, why should she move? Ann smiled and kissed him as if for a nice gesture.

"I'm not kidding. Take a few things and come along, this evening."

"What for?" Ann asked, unable to understand.

"Mother is not well," he lied.

"I can go and see her, but I won't stay overnight."

"Mother isn't sick, but I want you to come," George said.

Ann thought it was funny, like a good joke. She had no intention of moving and no matter how hard he tried he couldn't persuade her.

He stayed late, and it was hard for him to part with Ann: however, he said nothing about what had happened the day before. Without her noticing, he moved a house plant she kept in the room to the balcony, and asked her to sleep with her windows and balcony door closed.

Ann was working in a nursery school, and the next day she had to stay late. It had been agreed that George would pick her up about six o'clock.

On the way home, nothing seemed to remind him about the strange thing which had occurred. It was a summer evening, with clear skies. He walked through a park. The flowers were reveling among sprinkles of the water jets. Bright-colored flowers, with delicate stalks protected by green grass. The trees were bending over, friendly. The scenery was that of a fairy tale.

George was asking himself whether it was possible for all of these plants to hate man. Every argument was against it. They seemed to have been created for man's joy and delight, to remind him of beauty in his hours of weariness, after a workday spent to machines and papers filled with numbers. George saw the roses climbing up the wooden supports. "Maybe, plants dream of movement, that's why they roll up. Suppose they could walk, they would move to another place, and then another, sunnier, moister. Perhaps, their inability to move makes them hate us. They watch the daily motion about, but they must remain in place, waiting, day after day, spring after spring, for people's kindness. They are always at man's mercy, asking for his protection. Should the plants grow stronger than people, they would find a way to move. What else should they do with their strength? Why would they wish to destroy man? Wouldn't they rather fight boredom and ugliness?"

Thus, George was trying to find an explanation for yesterday's event. He made for home, weary and powerless. The flowers seemed to laugh at him.

Next morning in his office, he was working hard, wishing he couldn't remember anything. As for Ann, he didn't have to worry; they spoke over the phone. It was a hot day. The sun rays were coming through the window glass. Sometimes, clouds on the go would obstruct the light, but then the light would flow free again to the earth. It was stiffling hot, and a rain would be a true blessing. But no rain drop was in sight.

About ten o'clock an employee rushed into the office, gasping, pale. He leaned on the door, waived his hand and uttered with difficulty.

"The head accountant is dead."

Nobody said anything; everyone was waiting for the man to go on. But he collapsed.

Soon everybody knew; the head accountant died, choked by a plant in his office. Nobody had an explanation, because nobody was in his office when it happened; there was no scream. People were flabbergasted, and no one dared to go and have a look. What could they make out of that weird death? They were scared. They looked at the plants next to their windows: the plants were as calm and fresh as ever. George was the only one to have seen how such death occurs, but he dared not tell about what had happened.

About five o'clock he was home. His parents and a few neighbors were sitting around the table talking about people who had just died: people they knew, and people they didn't know. Anxiety and helplessness were taking over. Suddenly, a terrible scream came from the stairs, followed by others, begging for help. George tried to get out, but people in the room wouldn't let him. He looked at the flower on the balcony, and it seemed that its petals were growing and growing, ready to choke everyone. He saw blood flowing out of its tender petals in endless streams. Another desperate scream came from the street, bringing him back to reality.

The people in the room looked at each other. What were they supposed to do? Surely, they couldn't just sit around. George reached for the phone and dialed the nursery school where Ann was working. She told him that she heard talk about all kinds of strange happenings, but since she hadn't seen or heard anything, she wasn't scared. George promised to pick her up as soon as he could.

Suddenly, there was someone knocking loudly at the door. George made for the door, ready to open up. The others pulled him back.

"I must, I must!" he shouted and rushed to the door.

He opened up. On the threshold was a woman who had fainted from upstairs, the lip of a large, yet closed, leaf was piercing. The people in the room pulled the woman inside. Everyone seemed terrified. Screams of terror were coming from the street.

George decided to run to the nursery. His parents tried to stop him. However, he opened the door and went out. The people in the room ran to the window to watch him. He was walking slowly, carefully looking around. Suddenly, he heard his father's voice shouting:

"Run, George, run!"

He looked back in terror and saw a thick tree trunk rolling up toward him. It was reaching out, then rising over him, awesome. Instead of the limbs that probably had been cut off by lightning, a large, coal-black hole was looking at him.

George ran away, looking back now and again. Other people on the street saw the black giant and took off as well. George found himself by a lake. He hid behind a booth. A scream came from the lake. He saw a man swimming toward the opposite shore. Suddenly, water plants rose to the surface, surrounding him. Then, there was nothing more.

For a while, George remained motionless near the booth. The danger seemed to have passed. The tree trunk wasn't in sight anymore. He set off, slowly, carefully, heading to the nursery where Ann was waiting. The traffic was interrupted. He had to walk. The way seemed endless.

In the nursery's yard it was quiet. A few mothers were there to pick up their kids, and now they were setting off for home. George opened the door and entered a large hall, full of light, where children whose parents hadn't come were gathered. All around the room, next to large windows and on the stairs leading to classes, all kinds of plants, green and with blossoms, were motionless, filling the space with aroma beauty. Chairs were brought in, and the children sat down in a circle around Ann.

George sat on the window sill. Outside, he saw tree trunks, large leaves and long branches rising to the sky. The children were singing, along with Ann, a song about a scared mouse and shrewd cat. Sometimes the sky would get dark, and the children would look fearfully over the window. Ann would try to calm them down. The plants beyond the window were spying on what was going on in the room.

Then, a child rose, approached a flower which started turning toward the window and touched it. George rushed to the kid, but stopped halfway. The child was caressing the flower whispering:

"Now, be nice, be nice, I love you, I really do. Aren't you my own flower?"

George looked at Ann in surprise. The flower grew small again, and its petals were pointing to the boy, as if they were looking at him. The child took it by the stalk and brought it close to his face. Then he let the flower go and returned to his seat.

The children were whispering among themselves. Then, Ann started a fairy tale. The children grew silent. Outside, it was getting darker and darker. Ann was telling about fairies and dragons, brave children and ogresses. The children seemed to be listening. However, their eyes were looking beyond the windows to the plants that were covering the building. The plants were pointing their threatening trunks, coiling up like serpents, sprouting up like sky-bound lightning, hanging on the chimney, TV antennae, linking the telephone wires, knotting each other about. The sky, thus obstructed, grew darker and darker. From above, the petals of the oversized flowers were breaking off, flying over the streets and houses.

The children were sitting motionless. George and Ann met each other's terrified gaze. Ann asked the children to hold hands, and to listen to the tale. Her words, however, were mingling with the noise of trunks' movements and spasms, and were lost in the room, unheard. A child started crying, overcome with terror. The children had to be reassured somehow. They rose and ran to the window. Ann's voice made itself heard: "Back, children, back to your seats." She took them by hand and brought them to the middle of the room one by one. The children obeyed, but tears were running down their cheeks and now and then Ann's words were covered by screams of "Mommy, Mommy." Ann, speaking quietly, finally persuaded them that what was happening was a dragon's doing, and that Prince Charming will come at once and everything will be fine, and they were going to see the knight's face. The children believed her and calmed down. They were looking to the sky obstructed by big black plants and were waiting for Prince Charming to come.

Then Adrian, the bravest of the children rose again, approached his flower and told it:

"Go out and bring the daylight back. If you don't go, I will."

The flower rose to the ceiling.

Another child approached the flower and pulled the stalk down. The flower grew small again.

Without anyone's noticing, Adrian slipped away. The others saw him only after he appeared on the other side of the window. With his tiny hands, he pushed away the plants which had climbed up to the room. As soon as he would touch them, the plants would slip down, growing smaller. The children indoors were watching him fearfully, but the boy kept pushing, until the window lightened up again. All the way up, close to the sky, the plants kept on tossing about and clinging to each other. Adrian ran to the fence and touched every plant which had risen. He wanted to go through the gate, but Ann and George ran out to bring him back. Other children followed them outdoors. They caught up with him only at the crossroads. First scared, then insecure, the children would stop and, mimicking Adrian, touch the plants extended over fences and houses. They took heart, seeing the plants falling down, shrinking to their usual smallness. Up the street they went, one after another. Here and there they would stop and touch a plant, and the sky would grow bright.

Behind the children, the sunbeams broke through.

WHY DO FLOWERS CRY?

It looks like the white walls are all covered by shadows, and only one of them has a definite shape, and moves, and acquires a volume. The shadow approaches Maria and sits on the bed's edge. It strokes a lock of her hair, spread all over the pillow; it is silent. Maria would like to touch this shadow, to feel its hands, which she thinks are warm and trembling with emotion, to caress its pale cheeks.

Paul, the man with dark wavy hair and a high forehead, keeps silent and watches Maria. He doesn't say anything, for the shadows can't talk. His shape is constructed out of white-and-black volumes, which look bodyless, however; only his eyes look stronger than darkness and solitude, fill the room with the feeling of material existence. Paul's eyes have the color of embers, deep inside of which the fire is still burning. As if to keep the hidden flame from people, the dark embers stay protected by heavy eyelids, heavy with wearyness, although they might give the impression of quiet sadness.

Maria knows the spell of those eyes. Should she try to disturb the shadow, it would slide again along the wall and look at her, silent and cold, from the distant world of hope and illusion.

Outside it grew really dark. For almost three hours Maria has been waiting, patiently, for the shadow to disclose its thoughts, its words. But the telephone has been mute and indifferent like white-and-black shapes on the wall and Maria can only keep in mind the ember-like look half hidden by eyelids as if to keep some mystery from people.

Suddenly a thought gets into Maria's mind: to talk to the shadow. Perhaps it's not an illusion, but a live being, born out of Paul's soul.

"Why don't you talk to me?" Maria asks, in her mind, because she would find it strange to hear her own voice in a room where she was all alone.

The shadow stays motionless, looking at the young woman, dissolved in the strong beat of her own heart. Maria closes her eyes and reaches for the spot where she saw the shadow, saying, as if for herself:

"Where are you? You know how long I have been waiting for you."

Maria feels a hot touch, so hot and pleasant that she feels frightened that if she opens her eyes the heat will go away. She stands still, with only one thought in mind: "I love you."

"Do you love me?"

She could hardly hear the question. Paul's voice, slightly muffled, reverberates in her ears, and she feels his heart beating at times unbearably intense, at times almost fading.

"Do I love you? I do, as nobody did before. I know you don't believe me, I would like to prove it, but how?" says Maria as if she were repeating a well-memorized lesson.

Paul's voice cannot be heard any longer. Maria is alone, again. She opens her eyes. Paul doesn't watch her, and the wall is spotlessly white, with no shadows.

She becomes restless. It's late, and the telephone has been quiet for the whole day. It's Saturday, the day when the lonely souls hide in the corners of joyless rooms, filled with flickering hopes, sometimes born out of sheer fantasy. She turns on the tape recorder, and the shivering voice of a singer involved in his own unhappiness flows in, slowly, as if from a different world. In Maria's world there is only Paul, with his dark, wavy hair, pale face and searching eyes — searching for what?"

"Why don't you come?" asks Maria holding him and kissing his eyelids.

"Kissing eyelids means parting," says Paul.

"I know. But right now you are close. Hide your eyes behind your eyelids, I don't want you to lie to me any longer. Why don't you open your eyes? Why do your eyes look sad? What mystery are you hiding in the unseen part of your eyes? There, darkness means night, sadness. That's true. Where is the happiness I expected? Where is love, where is life?"

Maria knows that if he were here now he would tell her lots and lots of things. But she knew that it was useless to keep them, to fill her soul with them; still they kept tormenting her.

"Don't ask. Don't tell me you love me, I don't believe it. I'm afraid. I'm afraid, that one day you won't be here anymore, you won't want to be here."

Paul bends over the flowering plant next to the bed; from a petal, he catches, tears, and spreads it over Maria's hot cheek.

Maria opens her eyes. She looks at Paul, minute after minute, and then says:

"Do you know why flowers cry?"

Paul is silent.

"The flowers cry when people can't."

"Do you think these are tears?" asks Paul.

"They are my tears," says Maria, "they are tears of truth."

Paul touches her cheek and feels how hot it is.

"Don't cry," he says. "I don't trust women's tears. I don't trust anything. Anything of what you tell me."

Maria remains silent. She looks at the empty room and thinks that Paul doesn't know that flowers can cry.

The telephone rings. Maria gives a start. She runs to pick it up. The clock shows eleven. It's Saturday night, when all true lovers are together. She is frightened. Why? She is shivering, and she can hardly utter:

"Yes."

There is no answer at the other end. She knows it's Paul.

It's not the first time that he calls and then says nothing. Has he nothing to say? She could tell him so many things. Usually, she would insist. She would want to make him talk. Now, however, she hangs up and goes to bed.

It is dark in the room. A few rays of the moon come in from outside. Maria feels the white walls are covered by shadows, and only one shadow assumes shape, slides, acquires a volume; it approaches her, sits on the bed's edge, strokes a curl of her hair waving over the pillow, and says nothing.

NOCTURNE

The darkness is all over the beach. From far away comes the sounds of a slow tune. The sea moistens and freshens the air. That was a hot day. The hottest this summer. Two youths sit on a bench watching the endless horizon.

"I'm surprised Robert hasn't shown up yet," says one of them, the one with bright blue eyes.

"I haven't seen him in a long time. A couple of months ago I called on him. Do you know him well?"

"I learned about him here. He comes in the evening to the beach and stays here for hours. I know that his name is Robert and that he doesn't talk much."

His neighbor, a dark-haired youth with a short haircut and dark, calligraphically outlined eyes, has an absent look about him — for a moment. His gaze is projected into remoteness, onto some invisible point.

"When I last saw him. . ." he starts, and then he stops. He meets his friend's eyes.

"Go ahead," says the blue-eyed youth.

"When I last saw Robert, at his place, there was a girl there. She asked me to sit down. She had a sort of warmth about her, as if she were a very sensitive person, kind I'd say. 'How's Robert,' I asked. 'Fine. I think he's just fine,' she said, without conviction. 'Sometimes he's happy. He sleeps well.' 'Is he still restless?' I asked. The girl felt embarrassed. She didn't seem to know what to say. Her eyes fell to the ground. Then she said, in a low voice, 'Sometimes.'

"This means he hasn't quite forgotten.

"I remember him well. I hadn't seen him in a long time. I knew he was a quiet, very private man. He liked being all by himself. He was shy. In school, we used to call him 'the Poet.' His eyes, usually disturbingly quiet, would sometimes betray an inner restlessness. Should anyone ask about his problems he would say 'no problems at all.' Apparently he hadn't. He was a dreamer. He used to read a lot. He was interested in philosophy. According to him, in order to understand a philosophical truth one had to read all the controversies built around it. Then he took to science fiction. I know that he was a good student. He was successful, he liked his profession, he even loved it. Whatever he did, he took it seriously. When he came home he would stay by himself. He had no friends. Now and then, he had a visitor. I went to see him sometimes, without being asked. I would stay at the most one hour. Robert would keep silent. I had the impression I embarrassed him. I would leave then. I felt close to him. I think I loved him. One day I heard him telling me a strange story. It had been a long time since it had happened. It was like in his freshman year. . ."

The companion listened with interest. The youth fixed his eyes on something far beyond the shore. He stayed like that for a few seconds, then he went on.

"This was a marvelously lovely evening, in the month of May. The scent of flowers filled the town. Robert was living in a high-rise, on the ninth floor: he liked altitude. As a matter of fact, he still lives there. He has two rooms, rather small. He sometimes likes to stay with his lights off, watching the street and people. That evening, he put on a record, his favorite; it was Berlioz, the Fantastic Symphony. He sat down in the armchair, next to the balcony door. He leaned his head on the back. He looked at the sky, at the stars.

"He was thinking that everyone had a star of his own, and was wondering which one was his.

"His eyes were scanning the sky from one star to another. They stopped over on a weak, hardly noticeable star next to the Great Bear.

"'My star has got to be small, quite small. It would cling to the Great Bear, who is strong and can protect it. That will be my star, and when it disappears it shall die.'

"He looked at it again and smiled. Suddenly, he felt a slight breath of air. The record went off. He rose: he had to turn it over. And then. . .

"'I'm your star,' he heard.

"Robert stepped back. In front of him, on the balcony threshold, he saw her, his star. She had an organdy dress, all transparent; she had iridescent, blue eyes and white face, and

long hair, the color of blue summer sky, was covering her
shoulders.

"'Give me your hand,' she said. 'and don't be afraid. I'm
not a phantom. I'm your star. I watched you every evening.
You know,' she said, slightly touching his cheek, 'my name is
Star of Silence.'

"'Why?' Robert asked, hardly able to hear his own voice.

"'Because I talk very little. I am the littlest of my sisters.
So I let them speak.'

"Robert was wondering what he should do. He hardly
dared to look at her.

"'Let me turn the record over,' he murmured.

"The girl made a movement, and the music started
playing again. Robert looked at her. He said:

"'Now you are making miracles.'

"The girl laughed. Robert smiled.

"'Let's sit down,' she suggested.

"Robert didn't move. The girl took his hand and led him
toward the couch. They sat down.

"'As I see, you are even more silent than I am,' the girl
said.

"'I don't know what to say.'

"'Whatever you want. Tell me if you like me.'

"Robert considered. Then he said.

"'You are wonderful. I cannot believe this.'

"'What?'

"'That you are here. Will you come again?'

"'If you want me to.'

"She had a warm, rich voice. She was speaking slowly,
quietly. She looked at the sky.

"'I must go now,' she said quickly.

"Robert looked at the sky as well. The star next to the
Great Bear was missing. She was sitting next to him. She
rose. Robert kept sitting on the couch. She took his hands into
hers. She caressed them slightly. Then she disappeared. It
was dark in the house. Only a few rays came in from outside.
Robert looked at the sky. She was all the way up, again. His
heart sunk. Then he saw the star flickering. He smiled sadly.
He felt lonely. He lay on the couch. Now he could watch her.
The music was still playing. He felt he was going to fall
asleep.

"The next day, he was more pensive than ever. He was waiting for the evening to come. Indeed, she came again. They stayed together for a long time. The next evening, it was the same, and many evenings, month after month. Robert was happy. He told not a thing to anyone. He lost weight. He was sleeping little. He looked tired. One evening he sat in his armchair as usual. She came down. She was happy, she took his arm, they stayed close. Then she went to the mirror. Robert had a large mirror on the wall, next to the entrance door. The opposite wall was empty, except for a painting.

"'I want to ask you something,' she said.

"'Anything.'

"'Take this painting off the wall.'

"'You don't like it?'

"'I don't know. I hardly look at it.'

"Robert took down the painting. The star moved close to the wall.

"'Look in the mirror,' she said.

"Robert sat down on a chair in front of the mirror.

"'You are lovely,' he said.

"'Don't look at me. Look just at my reflection in the mirror. All right?'

"Robert nodded.

"'Do you want me to stay with you?'

"'I do,' said Robert.

"'I shall leave my soul here, next to this wall. You will be able to see me only in the mirror.'

"'And you will never come again?' Robert said fearfully.

"'Yes, I will.'

"The star came close to him, stroked him and kissed his hair. Robert looked in the mirror. He saw her next to him, and, in the mirror, against the wall, he saw her again. There were two of them.

"'What is this?' he said, frightened.

"'Nothing. The one in the mirror will stay with you until I die. Day and night. I shall come at night only.'

"Robert looked at her. She extended her arms and came close. She pressed her cheek against his. Stunning noise and blinding light filled the room. The star tore herself away from Robert's arm.

"'A lightning,' she said.

"Robert wanted to catch her hands again. A cloud was furiously wriggling through the room. The papers were blown away. The things were thrown to the ground. The doors opened. Robert wanted to catch Star's hand. She extended her arms pleadingly. The cloud covered her. The dust filled the room. He couldn't see anymore. Now and then, he perceived the pale sparkling of the Star: she was trying to free herself from the cloud's embrace. Robert heard her calling out. A rain started outdoors. The star wasn't in his room any longer. He looked up at the sky: it was covered by thick clouds. He went to the mirror, and there she was. She was leaning against the wall, silently, without moving. Now and then, little lights flickered through her hair.

"For several days the sky had been cloudly. One night, late, as he was standing in front of the mirror, Robert heard a strange noise coming from outside. Then he saw a light. He stepped out, onto the balcony: the sky was afire. He went back into the room and stood in front of the mirror. His star was there. He stood there holding his head between his hands. Later he fell asleep. He was awakened by a cry. Endless cry. The room was lit up by a lightning. He looked in the mirror. The shadow tore itself from the wall and came close.

"'Don't move,' she said.

"Robert started shivering. She stood, bodyless, next to the mirror. He felt something cold on his arm. He wanted to catch it, but it was transparent. A cold breath stroked his face. Robert looked into the mirror: she was hugging him.

"'Farewell,' he heard.

"Again, a lightning flew through the room. He looked in the mirror, and she wasn't there any longer. He looked at the wall, nothing. He rose, he tried to move back and forth through the room, he ran to the door. The sky was growing lighter. He waited for a few minutes. The sky grew clear. He looked at the Great Bear. He felt dizzy: the star wasn't there. She wasn't in the mirror either.

"'What do you know about her?' I asked the girl I saw in Robert's apartment.

"She let her eyes down. She looked at me, then at the mirror. Later, she said:

"'No one talks about her in this house.'

"I couldn't wait for Robert any longer, that day. He was too late."

They remained silent, both of them. The dark youth with vivid eyes took his friend's hand. One could hear someone coming.

"That's he," the youth said, in a low voice.

On the beach, there was a man's shape. It was Robert. He was walking quietly, with his head lowered. He was of average stature, and his hair had yellow lights lit by the moon. He was approaching the lighthouse. Then he disappeared. The two friends saw him again at a very top of the lighthouse. He was watching the sky.

TALKING TO NOBODY

Alex took the postcard and had a long look at it. It was a photograph featuring some spot of the world. Buildings, old and new, as in any other city, streets, broad and narrow, people, at the end of their working day, and the freshness of the air was enhanced by the trees, planted, a long time ago, and now sheltering a few plastic tables.

Alex took a magnifying glass and tried to tell silhouettes apart. He took a careful look at those sitting by the tables, then he lingered over those on the street, especially over a man, fortyish, wearing a beige coat, narrow tie and white shirt. The photograph caught him with his left foot slightly pushed forward, as if during a quiet, weary, or careless walk. Alex thought he had a strange gaze — lost, musing; he had short hair, and a pale and angular face. Alex brought the magnifying glass closer, and the man acquired shape and volume. Alex gave a start. He dropped the postcard on the table and started rummaging in an old box, which he had made of carved wood a long time ago. The box was full of photographs. He stopped, all excited, over one picture. Then he went to the table, took the magnifying glass, and his eyes darted several times, like an automation, from the picture card to the photograph and back. A look in the mirror finally convinced him: the man in the picture card was himself.

He took the card again and for a few minutes considered the structures. No, this spot was unknown to him, he never saw it before. Neither the front building, with carved roof edge, crowning the building royally; with tall windows on the facade, protected by gratings and thus giving the building the appearance of a castle; nor the high-rise on the right, with tall pillars, large, contemporary windows and the wall covered by a shiny chestnut-colored material. Nor the parasols, with their bright colors, nor pastic tables with their red-and-white checked tablecloths. He didn't know them. No. He has never been in that town.

Alex directed the glass to the street, and the man with the closely cropped hair and pale, angular face, asked him to sit at a table. Alex thought that was strange, but he didn't object. The people around them went on with their talk, only fragments of which could be heard. A background noise seemed to fill the air; the warmth of sunbeams coming through the parasols didn't tire them, and didn't muffle their vivid, strong voices. Alex and his twin sat face to face. The man didn't seem surprised by their being alike. Alex gave a start again. He realized he was dressed just like the other: beige coat, narrow tie, white shirt.

"I have a feeling I know you," said the pale-faced man.

"You must know me, since we are so much alike," murmured Alex.

"Why did you accept my invitation?"

"I felt like talking to someone. Why not you."

The pale-faced man smiled, with just the corner of his mouth. He seemed self-assured, his musing, lost stare grew clear and lively, and now, the only difference between them was the upbeat outlook of the stranger.

"What do you want from me?"

"I want you to tell me how to find happiness."

The pale man got lost in his thoughts. After a while, he said:

"What makes you think I know it?"

"Who are you, anyway?"

The stranger looked up to the sky. His eyes were shining, lightened by a sunbeam, his face blushed.

"Me?" he said surprised, "Don't you know me? I'm your vitality, your will of life."

"You're a liar!" Alex cried out. "I have no will of life, otherwise, I wouldn't be tormented by all those thoughts."

The man didn't answer. Then Alex went on in a lower voice.

"I feel lost. I don't want this shabby existence, with every moment resembling the past one. I want an explosion. I want to achieve something I have been failing for forty years. I want to create the work of my life, which would open a new age in the arts. I want to bend, religiously, in front of the creation, and kiss the brass cheek of a statue having your face, your vivid eyes.

Alex felt his face burning with excitement. He looked at the stranger and noticed that he was pale and musing again.

"What's the matter?" Alex said, worried.

"Nothing. I just gave you a little self-confidence and optimism, to make you able to dream, and to make your dreams come true."

"Do you think I shall ever be able to do what I want?"

"It depends."

"It depends on what?"

"On your talent and your confidence in it."

"I don't know whether I've got talent."

"Try, work, and see."

"I'm frightened," said Alex after a few seconds.

He kept silent for a while. Then he said, in a low voice, as if talking to himself, "I'm frightened. I'm frightened of the moment when I should learn I have no talent. I would kill myself. I cannot live anymore without achieving something great," he went on loudly. "I cannot live out of small stuff."

"Then all you have to do is to achieve your great work."

"Help me."

"How?"

"Stay with me."

"I'm always around. However, sometimes you get lost in details, and grow sad. Then, you don't notice me anymore, although I never go away. You will keep me, I promise, but I must ask you one thing: remember I am with you. Then you won't feel lonely. You will be able to work, to fulfill your wish."

"You know what? I really feel a desire to get down to work, I know I'll succeed, I feel a passion which tells me: don't linger, don't waste time. The brass statue with clear vivid eyes must come into existence, shine, bring joy."

Alex hasn't noticed that the chair in front of him was empty. The pale-faced man with clear, vivid eyes wasn't watching him any longer. Alex switched seats, so he would face the sun. He lifted his face toward the beams feeling how he blushes, how he smiles, how he laughs; his strong laughter covers the noises around. He gets up, and his steps carry him at a fast, dizzying pace, as if he were dancing.

A stunning noise makes him start. The magnifying glass falls from the table. He picks it up, brings it to his eyes and looks at the postcard. He fixes it over a man walking down the street, about forty, wearing a beige coat, narrow tie and white shirt, and he smiles at the man.

DUEL WITH THE SUN

I asked for a spade. I lifted it toward the sky. I decided to kill. I have to kill him to whom we owe our lives. Him who has subdued the Earth. I must kill his warmth. And the songs made for him. I must kill the Sun. He has stolen — deliberately and without hesitation.

This is not a game. Everything is real. I arranged my thoughts in a perfect order. I classified them, as carefully as any file clerk. I knew the power of each of them. I numbered them according to their strength; I compared them to the potentialities of life. Then I went out into the fields. I ran around, mad with joy. I ran and ran. While I was running over the green meadow I felt something strange happen. At first I thought that my compartments got mixed up. I checked. I was wrong. Something else had happened. My thoughts grew wings. So, I went after them. I caught them, but they told me: we aren't thoughts any longer. Surprised, I reprimanded them for disobedience. But I was fascinated: they became dreams. Large, powerful dreams, stronger than my will. I got frightened. I lost the reference of the reality. I could get lost in them altogether. They dominated me. "Where is my will?" I shouted. My will was standing, shy, in the middle of a blizzard of dreams. I was running in despair. I got somewhere close to the end of the Earth. There was a sea. One end of its endlessness. I slid over the waves. It welcomed me. The sea was glad to meet friends. I had the shrewd idea to quench my dreams in the sea. I couldn't. I was ashamed of myself and afraid of them. "As soon as I get back on the shore, they going to do me in," I thought. Perhaps, these dreams, stronger than thunder and earthquake are going to choke me. Then, I decided I was going to send them to the stars. The sea sensed my restlessness. He welcomed me with a carpet of water lilies. I have no idea where he got them, though I know he can do whatever he wishes. I sat on the carpet and I called the stars. They came out, one by one. Then I called my beloved. A lot of my dreams were for him. He came close. I looked into his green, clear eyes and told him my dream. He caressed me and disappeared. Then I felt a desire to leave nothing for the stars. However, I remembered something. I remembered the Earth and green eyes gone to other landscapes. The star looked at me with a smile and said: I'm going to keep your dreams. Give them to me. I can give them back to you any minute. She extended a white arm. She was like a fairy. I gave her my bunch of dreams, burning with love. I looked at them, flying to the sky. I called the star of fulfillments. Then, the star of friendships. And all the others. I looked at the sky. White fairies with silver crowns were carrying all of the colors of my dreams. I saw happiness. I had a long look at it. I only wished it would never stop. But it was only a short while. A short while, which was over. The stars disappeared. I looked around. I still was in the middle of the sea, on the lily-carpet. My heart was crying. I was alone. I thought the stars had deceived me. I felt like crying. I felt something burning me. Then, I saw that monstrous picture — sometime ago I would have thought it was divine. My greatest enemy was there. He drove away my stars. He was standing, triumphantly, in the illuminated sky. He extended his triumphant antennae towards me.He was laughing. "I'm going to kill you," I said. He just laughed. I thanked the sea and ran down the green meadow. The grass was boiling. It was furious, just like myself. People were out in the fields. I told them my story. They knew it. I got a spade. I'm going to get him, the Sun, I will. I wanted my dreams back. I want at least to see them in the hands of the Stars. And if Sun's power is greater than mine, if I won't be able to caress every moment the flowers held by Stars, then at least I want my dreams back. Here on Earth. They will submit to my will. I'll give them mine, I'll give them life. Why are you laughing? You are strong? I have the spade. My duel with the Sun will start in a moment.

THE SKETCH

He came home from the office. He wasn't tired. He sat down on the edge of the bed. He had been sitting like that for hours, thinking. It was getting dark. He didn't turn on the light. His eyes were fixed on the pattern of the plaid cover. But he couldn't see it. That's how Cornelia found him. She wasn't even sure he was thinking of anything in particular. She didn't want him to be upset. She turned on the light. Gabriel didn't move. She came close and kissed him. As usual, she asked:

"Are you upset?"

"No."

And that was the end of it. She left him alone and went to the kitchen: she brought some food. Gabriel rose and went to the window. He was looking and looking, remotelessly. He was dreaming of achieving something significant. He couldn't do it. First, to do what he wanted to, one needed talent. He had tried, but he himself had been disappointed. Why keep trying? For some time, he has been in a strange mood: sad, musing. He wouldn't take care of his apartment any longer: after coming home from work he would just throw his coat over the armchair and sit on the bed's edge. Or he would lie down, all dressed up, with his shoes on. He would lie, his hands under his head, looking up at the ceiling. It had been a long time since he last tried to read a book. The bookshelves were neatly set, as he had left them at the time when he would reach for a book now and then. He forgot he loved Cornelia. His love appeared to be something common, without interest. Sometimes he felt aggravated, when the girl asked too many questions. He felt like being alone, right now. He turned sharply. Noise came from the kitchen. He felt like being rude, throwing her out. By what right dare someone intrude into his life? However, it was so annoying, having to do something about it. So, he sat back on the bed, having turned off the light. The work didn't make him happy. Why live then? The others, so many of them, what were they living for? He didn't know. They could have their reasons, each of them. Or they didn't bother to ask themselves the question. He felt he couldn't live like that any longer. Should he kill himself? He was going to die someday, anyway. What should he live for? He could have asked, for whom should he live. He dared not. He was running away from people. He was thinking that otherwise, people might run away from him. And why shouldn't they. Could he teach them anything? Nothing. Then, why should they accept him as a friend? He rejected the question. He was feeling useless. The thought of death would come back, day after day, but he couldn't do that. He couldn't kill himself. Somewhere, deep down beneath all of the tormenting thoughts there was a hope. A tiny, deep-hidden hope — but it was there. Perhaps, he will be able to create something. He had tried, but he was afraid to do it again.

That evening, he was sadder than ever. He couldn't believe he would achieve anything in life. He made up his mind: he had to kill himself. There was nothing to stop him. A bit of courage — and that will be it. His face was tense; it had a strange, cold expression. The thought of death couldn't scare him. Perhaps they will think him a coward. Why a coward? Everybody will die. To live purposeless, to crawl along — wasn't that a bigger cowardice? His decision grew stronger.

"Why did you turn the light off? I made some food," Cornelia said. She turned on the light. Gabriel roared. Scared, Cornelia turned it off almost automatically. She opened the kitchen door to let some light in, and came closer to him. He was lying, motionless. She laid her hand on his forehead.

"You've got a fever," she whispered. Gabriel pushed her away and rose.

"Go away, right now," he yelled. Cornelia was terrified. She leaned on the door. He came closer and held out her coat. Then he returned to his bed. He leaned his head on his hands, looking down where Cornelia stood for a while at the door; she wanted to come closer. Without a movement, he said again:

"Go."

She looked at him: her eyes grew moist. Then she left. Now, Gabriel was only wondering: should he or shouldn't he leave her a note, so she will understand why he had to die. He decided against it. She couldn't understand, anyway. He went to the bathroom. He thought it was proper to wash first. He threw some water on his face, took the towel and wiped himself. He saw his face in the mirror. He was handsome. Large, black eyes; short chestnut hair; fine-shaped nose; virile oval; strong jaw. "Pointless," he thought. He threw away the towel and took the razor. As he was ready to reach for the vein, he remembered the dream. He could try. For the last time. He threw the razor. It took much less time to choose to live. This night he will try again. Now he had to run to find the paints. As he was taking his coat, he felt a hand on his shoulder. He looked to the right. There was a young man. Just like himself. He seemed to have the same age. The same body, the same face. His eyes were livelier, though. And he had a slightly ironical smile. He looked self-assured   a man capable of giving orders. They sat down opposite each other. The newcomer was wearing a narrow-fitting T-shirt. Gabriel watched him in surprise. The man broke into laughter. A hearty one. Gabriel felt aggravated.

"Who are you?" he uttered. He wouldn't move. In fact, he realized he couldn't move.

"Your death," the guest said, smiling.

"Hum!"

"You don't believe me? It's true."

"Where were you up to now? Why shouldn't you come when I called you?"

"I existed within you. Now I came precisely because you don't want me anymore."

"You come when you're not wanted?"

"Sometimes. But I came because *you* don't want me. I hadn't wanted you to meet me. You were ready to be mine. You changed your mind, stupidly, at the last moment. As I was one step short of victory."

"You can overcome whenever you wish."

"Not really. It's hard, fighting life. Especially when dealing with young people. And you must know, I like you better for beeing young. You see, I have your face. Do you think wrinkled would become me?"

"You're pale, however."

"I am, for I live in darkness.'

"What do you want?"

"Nothing."

"Why have you come then?"

"To see your torment. To see your failing. To see your wishing that I come. Becoming my friend."

"You think I shall fail?"

"Without me, you will. In fact, you had."

Gabriel kept in mind his failures. He was ready for help. They sat at the table.

"I cannot make you a celebrity. I can give you all the talent you want.I can bring you man's appreciation. You will be the greatest artist."

"What are you asking in exchange?"

"Almost nothing. Your life. Don't be afraid. Not now. You can work; I give you everything. I let you do whatever you want. You can open an exhibition. A huge one —everyone will admire you. However, the next day after the opening, after you have become a great man, you must give me your life. Bear this in mind: otherwise you won't be able to do anything. As an old man, you'll feel sorry you hadn't listened to me."

Gabriel was silently considering.

"If you say no, I shall leave. I won't bother you any longer. You will be left alone. One day you're going to call me again. Then, I shall not repeat this offer. I shall be content with your corpse. You will give me this gift."

"You promise me absolutely everything?"

"Everythng."

"Including talent?"

"Including."

"And fame?"

"As well. The day you open your exhibition, everyone will love you. Newspapers will be writing about you. On the radio, they will be talking about you."

"No. I only want you to give me one thing: talent. People will see my paintings and grow kinder and lovelier. My work will convey beauty. I want them to need me, that's all. Not famous — loved."

"Do you accept?"

"I accept."

Death extended his hand.

"Write here; that's right, with your finger."

On Death's hand a "yes" appeared, written in blood.

"Now start working," the white-dressed man said. I am going to lie down for a while. I like looking at you."

They rose to their feet. Death made a movement with his head. In the corner of the room, an easel appeared. Next to it, a small table, with all kind of paints, and brushes. On the chair, a navy smock. Gabriel took off his coat and shirt. On top of his undershirt, he put the navy smock. Then he took the paint tubes and mixed the paints. He took a sketch and fixed it on the easel. Then, he took a pencil and started drawing a portrait of the newcomer. He was looking at his model, lying, his hands under his head, as he, Gabriel, used to lie. He decided to make Death's face more colorful — he didn't care for a corpse-like complexion. The work was coming out fine. He succeeded in doing exactly what he wanted. He was content. He liked Death's eyes; they had a familiar design. Their expression however! It was unusual, fascinating. He wondered why was it that Death had a livelier face than himself did."

"Would you like something to eat?"

"Don't be silly. I feed only on your disenchantments."

"Now I have none."

"You've fed me well enough so far."

Gabriel went to the kitchen. He had a snack. He felt sucha hunger for life.

Several days passed by, and he painted and painted. Then, he decided he wanted to paint outdoors. Somewhere, in the mountains. On the grass.

"You are free," Death said, "you can go."

Gabriel packed his paints and brushes and folded the easel.

"Are you coming along?"

"Without me, you have no chance."

"Aren't you cold?"

"Never."

"What do you think people will say when they see you dressed like that?"

"Nobody will see me but you."

They left. They took a train — the first they could catch.
Gabriel was cheerful. He was looking out of the window. The
fields, in front of him, bore the pale colors of Autumn. The
trees were heavy with fruit. A bountiful Fall! Gabriel felt in
his heart a joy unutterable. Never did the field seem the same.
Never were the trees so magnificent. Never were the sunbeams so bright. He was thinking he was going to show all of
this on the canvas. These images were to live, in everlasting
glory, through his colors. The canvas will be life. The life that
he would like to enjoy forever. He was wondering, if the trees,
the fields and the sun had always been as splendid as that
moment, and why he had never realized that.

The train followed its meandering way among the
mountains. He must get off. At one of the next stations. He
took his luggage and made for the door.

"I am going to be where you will choose to stop."

"Why aren't you coming along?" Gabriel asked.

"The sun bothers me."

And he disappeared. Gabriel felt good. He thought it was
stupid to complain about the sun. Especially since it wasn't
exceedingly hot. Ah, well. What difference did it make. He
had the most precious thing — his talent. He needed nothing
else. Now he only had to work. This was his dream — the
dream that kept him alive. The dream that had to come true.
He set off, up the mountain path. In a short while, he found a
sunny clearing. He put down the easel and the paints,
approached a beech tree and put his arms around it. He looked
at the sky — it was high, high above him. He turned around
the tree. It looked as if the tree started turning its crown,
faster and faster. It was like a game the beech was playing
against the heavens. The tree was robust, tall, opulent.
Gabriel recorded the image of the rotating crown. He went to
work. On the canvas, the leaves blazed trails against the sky.
The trunk was powerful, solemn. He liked the idea of power.
It came to his mind that if he climbed the tree he would have
proven more powerful than the old wooden giant. He decided
that he was. On the sky, he drew a man. The man's hand
reached for the trunk and bent it. Gabriel liked that.

"There you were!"

"Where else? Now that you're here, I'm going downhill to
look for a room. I'll leave all the stuff here."

"Don't worry, No one will steal it."

Down the hill he saw a house — a lovely house,with a sunporch. He knocked. A stout woman came out.

"I would like to rent a room for a couple of months."

"Sure. I've got two rooms: one is for my husband and myself, the other I could rent out. Are you alone?"

"No. That is, yes. Alone."

For the first time, Gabriel knew what it meant being happy. He would wake up early and go uphill. Or else, he would stay on the porch. Sometimes, he went to the station, or to the sheepfold. He painted about a dozen paintings. He was content. The peasant woman kept marveling at how beautiful they were. The weather was sunny. Winter was over. Then Spring, and Summer. It was never too cold, or too hot.

He told Death it was time to go home. They left. The room back home was the same as he had left it. He put the easel in the same corner. His mind was filled with new impressions, he could start working again. Death sat on the bed as before.

Gabriel decided it was time to review his work. He put a painting on the easel, sat on the armchair and took a long look. Then he asked.

"Do you like it?"

"People will think it's wonderful."

The mountains were standing, in all their majesty, in front of him. He almost felt he could climb them. They had volume and color of the real mountains.

"Do you think I could tear off a fir twig?"

"Try."

Gabriel rose and approached the easel. In front of him, there was a real mountain. He touched the fir tree. Itw as real. He tore off a branch and returned to his place, next to the bed.

"You're strong."

"The strength is in your painting now."

Gabriel looked at the painting. A fir tree had a broken branch. He approached the painting again and put the branch back into its place. Then he put the canvas down and took another one. This was the one with the tree turning against the sky. Somebody knocked at the door. Gabriel opened it.

There were two fellow workers who he hadn't seen for a year.

"Hi, Gabriel."

"Hi."

"Why didn't you come to work?" one of them asked.

"I am working. No, don't sit on the bed," he shouted; the men looked surprised. "Sit on the chairs."

"Say, Gabriel, who made this?" asked the blond one, getting closer to the easel.

"Don't get closer," said Gabriel, "sit down. Do you like it?"

"A wonder."

They were looking in silence, motionless.

"That's it. Now, the next one." said Gabriel with a smile. He changed the canvas.

Having shown all the paintings, Gabriel looked at his visitors. They were sitting silently, with the same attitude. They looked as if they were waiting.

"More," the blond man said in a low voice.

"I have no more."

"Listen, Gabriel, you mean they are yours?" the other uttered.

"Yes."

"Gabriel, you now who you are? You know what you are? Man, you're a genius!"

Gabriel was happy. His friends left; they said nothing else. While leaving, they looked into his face as if they wanted to remember it forever.

"I must go," Gabriel told Death.

"Where?"

"To look for an exhibition room"

"You won't work anymore?"

"After I'm back. In two months I want to open an exhibition."

"Take a painting with you."

Gabriel left. However, he was soon back.

"I have the room."

"I know."

"How?"

"I was with you. I told you, without me you can get nothing."

Gabriel got back to work. As soon as he had twenty paintings he took them to the exhibition room. He forgot about the contract. He didn't care anyway. He wanted people to enjoy his work. He packed the paintings by five and tied each pack with a string. Then, he fixed five on his chest and five on his back; he carried the others under his arms. It was twilight. A wind started blowing. The street was almost empty — one or two passers-by here and there. He walked with difficulty, but firmly. He had one sight in mind: the opening; people lingering in front of each painting; he, hidden in a corner absorbing the emotion. The room, converted to a hearth of beauty, and he — the one lighting up a flickering light in everyone's heart.

The wind was growing stronger. He had more and and more difficulty advancing. The sky was dark with clouds, the trees were bending low. The tin roofs of houses were vibrating. The paper scraps had been blown from the sidewalk. The dust obstructed his eyes. The wind's power amplified, more and more. He couldn't see any longer. He kept going, his eyelids almost closed. He heard the wind's whistle in his ears. And the sound of broken windows. The paintings were swinging against him. The string was ready to yield. Gabriel tried to hurry. Useless. A power stronger than the wind was hindering his step.

"Where are you?" he shouted in despair.

"I'm here."

"Help me out."

"The wind is stronger than I am. You have to struggle by yourself. I am hiding within you. You're the one who has life in him; you have will, you can fight."

Gabriel kept walking. Foot after foot, with enormous strain. His clothes were torn. He was holding the paintings with both hands. A new gust of wind came. The string attaching the front and back paintings broke. The paintings were sliding down the sidewlk. He jumped to stop them, and got a hold on two of them — he couldn't hold any more. At least he should save those two he was thinking. He was holding them tight. The hurricane was still unyielding. He tried to run, he couldn't. Easy, easy, I'm going to make it, he kept thinking. The hurricane grew wilder. It pulled the other five paintings away from his hands. Gabriel turned around

ana watched them fly away. They fell on the ground, then
took off again. He still had seven more. He had to save them.
He set off. A new gust — and he was thrown to the ground,
face down. The paintings were snatched away. He reached
with his hands to catch them. They turned about him, but he
couldn't catch hold of them. He rose to his knees. He noted
two people passing by. They were his visitors. He called
them: they looked at him and he pointed to the paintings; they
went their way. He shouted for help. People gathered around
him. A shower broke out. Gabriel looked at the only painting
that was still close. It was Death's portrait. He tried to reach
it; he couldn't. He asked people for help — there was no one
around anymore. He was all alone. His eyes were fixed on the
last painting. The rain was ruining the lines. He rose to his
feet. Now and then people would pass by — indifferent. He
made for home. The rain went on.

"Now I can come with you," he told Death who was
walking along.

"No. The deal is out. I have been paid enough; have you
seen all those people? No one would help you. It's them you
wanted to work for? To achieve — for them?"

"No longer. They don't deserve it."

"I don't need your corpse. I need your soul. Now your
soul is mine. It is dead, even though you're alive. This is my
meaning. This is what feeds me. It's more than a poor body,
be it even young."

Gabriel said nothing more. Death was now within him.
Should he kill himself or stay alive — it was Death's victory
either way. At home, he sat on the bed's edge, as usual, and
took his head in his hands, his eyes looking down.

The entrance door opened. He heard steps. It was
Cornelia. She took off her coat and turned on the lights.

"You have been sitting like that since yesterday?" she
asked cheerfully.

Gabriel looked at her. He remembered her.

"What do you mean, since yesterday?" he asked, "I
haven't seen you for one year."

"What's wrong with you, Gabriel darling? Yesterday
you pushed me out. I came now because I new you were sick.
It's such a terrible rain outside. Cats and dogs. Look, Gabriel,
see what I found?"

She went to the entrance and came backwith a sketch. Gabriel gave a start. He took it and looked at it.

"Where did you find it?"

"The wind threw it against a wall."

"Cornelia, this sketch. . ."

"It's magnificent. Some great artist must have done this. I am not into it, but I can see that. It's a shame the rain damaged it. But it's a master's hand."

"You mean it?"

"What's so surprising?"

"Cornelia," Gabriel said. Then he remained silent. They looked at the painting, both. Then he rose and put the sketch by the book-case. Again, he sat on the bed next to the girl. "Cornelia, this sketch is mine."

Cornelia gave him a large, surprised look.

Gabriel went to the easel. He started drawing that tree set against the sky.

TO OUR READERS: We welcome inquiries about our publications. In case your bookstore does not have this particular publication of ours that you desire, please order directly from us by mail, enclosing the list price plus $2.00 for mailing and handling.

Brunswick Publishing Company
Route 1, Box 1A1
Lawrenceville, Virginia 23868

DATE DUE

Here We Go!

Helena Pielichaty

WALKER BOOKS

For my super editors, Caz Royds and Annalie Grainger, who've supported Girls FC from kick-off to final whistle. Thank you so much.

First published 2012 by Walker Books Ltd
87 Vauxhall Walk, London SE11 5HJ

10 9 8 7 6 5 4 3 2 1

Text © 2012 Helena Pielichaty
Cover illustration © 2012 Sonia Leong

The right of Helena Pielichaty to be identified as author of this work has been asserted by her in accordance with the Copyright, Designs and Patents Act 1988

This book has been typeset in Helvetica and Handwriter

Printed and bound in Great Britain by Clays Ltd, St Ives plc

British Library Cataloguing in Publication Data:
a catalogue record for this book is available from the British Library

ISBN 978-1-4063-1733-6

www.walker.co.uk

☆ ☆ The Team ☆ ☆

☆ Megan "Meggo" Fawcett GOAL

☆ Petra "Wardy" Ward DEFENCE

☆ Lucy "Goose" Skidmore DEFENCE

☆ Dylan "Dyl" or "Psycho 1" McNeil LEFT WING

☆ Holly "Hols" or "Wonder" Woolcock DEFENCE

☆ Veronika "Nika" Kozak MIDFIELD

☆ Jenny-Jane "JJ" or "Hoggy" Bayliss MIDFIELD

☆ Gemma "Hursty" Hurst MIDFIELD

☆ Eve "Akky" Akboh STRIKER

☆ Tabinda "Tabby" or "Tabs" Shah STRIKER/MIDFIELD

☆ Daisy "Dayz" or "Psycho 2" McNeil RIGHT WING

☆ Amy "Minto" or "Lil Posh" Minter VARIOUS

Official name: Parrs Under 11s, also known as the Parsnips

Ground: Lornton FC, Low Road, Lornton

Capacity: 500

Affiliated to: the Nettie Honeyball Women's League junior division

Sponsors: Sweet Peas Garden Centre, Mowborough

Club colours: red and white; red shirts with white sleeves, white shorts, red socks with white trim

Coach: Hannah Preston

Assistant coach: Katie Regan

☆ ☆ Star Player ☆ ☆

☆ **Age:** 10

☆ **Birthday:** 2 February

☆ **School:** Mowborough Primary

☆ **Position in team:** Goalkeeper

☆ **Likes:** football, hot chocolate with marshmallows, football, especially women's matches on TV

☆ **Dislikes:** long school assemblies, burnt pizza, wet playtimes

☆ **Supports:** England, England Women, the Parrs

☆ **Favourite player(s) on team:** Haven't really got one

☆ **Best football moment:** Winning the Nettie Honeyball cup

Megan "Meggo" Fawcett

☆ **Match preparation:** warm-up, deep breathing exercises

☆ **Have you got a lucky mascot or a ritual you have to do before or after a match?** I wear the red bandana Hannah Preston, my old coach, gave me.

☆ **What do you do in your spare time?** Hang out with my mates, play with Whiskas, my cat.

☆ **Favourite book(s):** Keeper by Mal Peet. I read loads of magazines, too, such as Match.

☆ **Favourite band(s):** Rebecca Ferguson, Adele

☆ **Favourite film(s):** Hugo

☆ **Favourite TV programme(s):** Take it Like a Fan

Pre-match Interview

Hello. My name is Megan Fawcett and I'm the goalie for the Parrs Under 11s, the best girls' football team in the world. Like I said in my last Pre-match Interview, don't worry if you've never heard of us. I won't be offended. Perhaps you've never heard of Donny Belles or Dick, Kerr's Ladies either? Nothing would surprise me.

Anyway, I'm going to finish the series by telling you what happened to the Parrs when half our players left because they got too old and we needed to recruit new ones. It didn't turn out like I'd imagined but then nothing ever does in football, does it? That's what makes it so brilliant.

Love and penalty saves,
Megan F xxx

WANTED

Girls aged 8–11 to join
awesome football team the
Parrs Under 11s (winners of this
year's Nettie Honeyball cup)

Training every Tuesday at
Lornton FC ground

Fun open day will be held on
Saturday 7 June at Lornton FC

Email slewisparrsfc@gmail.com

1

"Ta muchly, Tabs," I said as I gathered Tabinda's shot safely in my arms.

Tabinda scowled and jogged back down the field while I surveyed my options. Dylan was tracking back down the left wing and Petra down the right. Normally I'd have directed my goal kick at one of them but not this time. This time they were the opposition. I aimed straight down the middle of the pitch for Daisy instead.

"Nice one, Megan."

I turned to see Mr Glasshouse, our head teacher, smiling at me. He had three chubby infants clinging to him like toffee apples to cellophane. "Hi, Mr Glasshouse," I said.

"What's the score?"

"Five–nil to us, so far."

"Excellent. Glad to see you keeping a clean sheet."

"Only because Year Six is out and JJ's in detention."

He sighed. "Ah, my precious Year Sixes, looking round their new secondary schools. We'll miss them, especially Connor. He's such a top-class keeper."

"Yes, I know."

"I don't know what we'll do without him."

"You'll be fine, I'm sure."

"Well, we might be. I've heard there's an exciting prospect in Year Five. Brave, too. Rumour has it she broke her nose making a save once."

"Mr Glasshouse, you're doing that thing again."

"What thing?"

I craned my neck to see where the ball was. "Dropping hints about me coming to play for school."

"OK, I'll stop dropping hints and ask you right out. Do you fancy being my goalie next year?"

"I can't. There's only one team in my life and that's the Parrs."

"I don't mind sharing."

"I do! By the way, we're after new players, too, so if you know anyone interested we've got an open day on Saturday. All welcome."

"Excuse me, I'm the one doing the poaching here."

I laughed and was about to say something else when I saw that Tabinda had filched the ball from Daisy and was speeding towards me. Nobody seemed to be trying to stop her, either. "Close her down, then, someone!" I ordered, moving forward to narrow the angle, then bouncing on my feet and watching, watching all the time.

Tabinda, over-zealous now, dropped her right shoulder and had a shot. I flung myself to the ground and punched the ball away, straight into Dylan's path. Dylan, caught by surprise, wellied it over the goal and almost knocked out one of Mr Glasshouse's tiddlers. It was the last action of the match. By the time I'd collected the ball it was full-time or, as some people call it, the end of lunch.

Everyone splintered into small groups and headed towards school. I fell in with Tabinda and Petra.

"Five–nil. That's appalling," Tabinda complained, tossing her plait over her shoulder in disgust.

"How come you always guess right? Like when Tabs shot just then?" Petra asked as we went inside.

"What can I say? I'm a genius."

She laughed. "And so modest."

"Let's wait for the twins," I said, glancing over my shoulder. "I want to ask them if they're going to the open day."

It took a while for them to catch up with us. They were ambling across the field, heads together, engrossed in their conversation. They looked startled when they realized we were waiting for them.

"Hey, Meganini," Dylan said.

"Hey, Dyl. Hard lines on that last shot."

Dylan shrugged. "I bestruddled it instead of being delicate."

"Exactly. You're getting closer every time, though.

Who knows – maybe you'll replace Eve as top
striker next season, eh?"

The twins exchanged stricken glances, then
Daisy nodded towards Dylan, and Dylan swallowed.
"Meganini?" she said.

"Uh-huh?"

"We've got something to tell you."

"OK."

"Daisy and I aren't going to do winging any more."

"What, during lunch?"

"No. For the Parrs at Parsnip time."

"The thing is," Daisy continued quickly, "we've
enjoyed our football phase, but we've just read the
highly wonderful book by Mrs Noel Streatfield called
Ballet Shoes and so we thought we'd give ballet
a go next, and ballet attendance times clash with
football attendance times."

"Ballet?" I spluttered. "You'd give up footy for
soppy ballet?"

Dylan nodded. "Yes. We think we'll look adorable
in tutus."

I was speechless.

"You're not cross with us, are you, Meganini?" Dylan asked. "We'll still play football at lunchtimes."

"No," I sighed. "I'm not cross."

Daisy and Dylan both looked relieved. "I'd hate it if you were in a frump with us. You're our" – Dylan began counting on her fingers – "fourth best friend."

"Thanks," I said.

"No worries, girlfriend." Dylan beamed and they skipped off, leaving the three of us to stand there and stare.

JJ just shrugged when I told her about it during afternoon registration. "Well, they've always been like that, haven't they? Unpredictable."

"I know but..."

I didn't have a chance to say any more. Mrs Marston, our boring stand-in teacher, slapped a booklet down on the table in front of JJ. "Your report book, young lady," she said coldly. "I'd aim for a good start in it if I were you."

I'd have been mortified, but JJ was a report-book veteran. She didn't even flinch.

Still, it did the trick and she behaved all through CDT and Music. She was even perfect during silent reading at the end of the day. Now me, I'm not so good at silent reading, not in classrooms anyway, so I did fake silent reading instead and let my mind drift. Naturally it drifted towards the twins' news.

We were down to four players. *Four*. What if no one else joined? We wouldn't have a team. That couldn't happen. I only had one season left in the Under 11s myself. I wanted to go out with a bang, not a whimper.

2

"Oh, hello, what's with the long face?" Dad asked when I got in from school. "Decimal fractions for homework again?"

I flopped down in the armchair opposite him. "No. Worse than that. The twins are dropping out of the Parrs."

Dad pointed the remote at the TV and turned down the sound on the cricket commentary. "What? No twins? Aw, that's a blow."

"It's not a blow, Dad, it's a disaster. Get it right."

"Ah, a disaster. Like the sinking of the *Titanic*. I stand corrected."

"Do you think I should phone Hannah?"

"Hannah? Why?"

"To tell her the news."

"I would have thought if you were going to call

anyone it should be Sian." Sian is our new coach. She took over from Hannah and Katie at the end of last season.

"But Sian doesn't know the twins like Hannah does. The McNeils aren't like normal families, are they? Hannah will know what to do." My heart leapt at the thought of hearing her voice. I hadn't talked to her since the presentation evening and that was weeks ago.

Dad's heart didn't leap, though. Not even a flutter. "Listen, Fishface, we've discussed this. You've got to let the poor girl get on with her life. She'll be snowed under preparing for teacher-training college. The last thing she wants is to be bugged about the McNeils. Leave her alone."

"But—"

"No, Megan. You've got to stop relying on her. She's not the coach any more."

"I know. I just..."

"And didn't she ask you to be as supportive as possible with Sian? To help her all you could?"

"Yes and I have been. I've made a list of all the things she needs to know."

"Great. Then add 'The twins have left the team' to the list."

"Fine," I mumbled. "I'll add it to the list."

"Good girl." Dad beamed at me. "And yes, I'd love a cup of tea. Thanks for asking."

So I made Dad a cup of tea and then I went upstairs and added "Twins leaving" beneath "Types of players needed" and "Who to watch out for in the league". After that I sulked a bit about the Hannah thing, then came downstairs to play with Whiskas, my cat. I can't say it was the most exciting evening I've ever had but, hey, it was a school night.

The trouble with school nights is they're followed by school days. As usual, in the morning, our classroom was noisy and Mrs Marston was nowhere to be seen. About ten kids on the far table were playing rucksack rugby. It was the newest craze. For three points you had to chuck your backpack or rucksack across an entire table without it knocking over any pencil pots or equipment. You weren't allowed a forward pass. Whoever touched the rucksack down on Mrs Marston's desk was the winner. Unfortunately, JJ always seemed to manage to touch the bag down on Mrs Marston's desk at the exact moment Mrs Marston walked in, hence the detention and report book yesterday.

I half expected to see JJ in the thick of it today, but she was sitting at our table quietly reading a book. It was as if she'd stayed in the same position overnight, only the book had changed. "What are you reading this time?" I asked.

She quickly covered it with her hands. "Nothing."

"It's *Ballet Shoes*. I recognize the cover," Petra said.

"Jenny-Jane Bayliss, reading a book on ballet?" I teased.

JJ sniffed. "I wanted to see what was so special it would make the twins ditch footy," she said.

Mrs Marston bustled in then, throwing her heavy

leather handbag on the desk with a thwack. Her eyes immediately focused on JJ, but she couldn't find any fault, so she began shouting at the rugby players instead. I sighed and reached for my tray. Roll on lunchtime, I thought.

That was pretty much it for the rest of the week. Boring old school made bearable by footy at lunchtimes. I tried my best to persuade the twins to come to the open day, but apparently they were having their first ballet lesson then. They promised me their mum had phoned Sian about leaving and Sian had been fine about it. I sighed and crossed that "To do" from my list.

The other disappointment was Eve couldn't come, either, nor could Nika or Lucy. I'd hoped they'd be there for old times' sake, but it seemed Saturdays in June were busy, busy, busy. "We're thinking of going to this at the end of August, though," Eve said, handing round flyers her form teacher, Mrs Hulley, had picked up and thought they'd be interested in.

"What is it?" I asked.

"Only the biggest women's football fixture of this century, dude. England at home to the USA. It's a friendly, but it's still going to be a-ma-zing."

"I am so going to that," I said, snatching the flyer from her hand.

"Thought you might." Eve grinned.

I tucked the flyer into my pocket to save for later. I had my own little team of internationals to think about first.

3

The morning of the open day was glorious. Bright sunshine, clear blue sky. Perfect weather. I got dressed in jeans and my Parrs home shirt, then I made Dad a cup of tea. Mum was on the early shift at the hospital and already at work or I would have made her one, too, in case you were wondering.

We called for Petra en route and arrived at Lornton FC just before ten. I was so keen to see Sian, I didn't even say hello to Auntie Mandy in the clubhouse first. "Tell her I love her and I'll be round to eat all her biscuits later," I instructed Dad.

"And crisps," Petra added.

"Glad to see those lessons on healthy eating are making an impact." Dad chuckled and waved us off.

☆ ☆ ☆

I told Petra my team wish list as we headed for the training field behind the clubhouse. "A couple of solidly built girls to support us in defence. Two or three midfielders. Someone with Eve's instinct for the net would be a bonus, and if we find anyone half as good as Gemma..."

"...Result!"

"Result times ten."

JJ was leaning against the bottle bank waiting for us. Like me, she was wearing her Parrs shirt, but unlike me she was also wearing a scowl deeper than the Cheddar Gorge. "What's wrong?" I asked.

"Nothing," she mumbled and led the way towards the pitch, hands tucked into her jeans pockets.

I didn't know what was up with JJ. I thought everything looked great. There were red and white striped gazebos with various banners and advertising hoards outside each one, lining the near side of the pitch. An ice-cream van was parked to the left of the away goal, a bouncy castle to the right. The smell of fresh coffee and doughnuts wafted across the field from a marquee on the far side of the field. People were already sitting at the plastic tables alongside it.

The pitch itself was set out with what looked like every piece of training equipment we had. Rows and rows of it; cones and skipping ropes, slalom posts and hoops. Bang in the middle was one goal with a net of footballs leaning against the near post.

So this was what an open day looked like. "Wow," I said.

"All it needs is Splat the Rat and it could be the May Fair." Petra laughed.

JJ just grunted.

"Look, isn't that Tabs?" I asked. Over by the bouncy castle, Tabinda and her dad were chatting to a girl and a guy wearing a beanie hat and heavy sports coat. The girl had her head bent, examining her feet. I'd seen the two of them somewhere before, but couldn't remember where. Tabinda waved. She said something to her dad, then came bounding over with the girl in tow. "Hey, everybody, do you remember Serena? Cuddlethorpe Tigers?"

Serena, small with dark hair held back by a white headband, looked uncomfortable. "Hi," she said, her glance taking us in hurriedly before resting back on her feet.

"I thought I recognized you. You've got that amazing long throw-in," I said, mentally ticking "midfielder" off my wish list.

"And that dad who shouts a lot," JJ added.

"JJ!" I said and dug her in the ribs.

Serena shrugged. "Don't worry about it. It's true. On both counts." It turned out her dad was the reason she was here. He felt she was wasting her time at Cuddlethorpe because they'd finished seventh out of ten in the league.

"We were only fourth," I pointed out.

"But you won the cup. That counts for a lot in his book."

"Do you want to leave Cuddlethorpe?" JJ asked.

"Not really," Serena admitted.

"Don't, then," JJ told her. "'Cos we won't be winning diddly-squat this season."

"How do you know that?" Petra asked crossly.

"I've seen who's signing up, that's how," JJ retorted.

"What do you mean?" I asked.

"Tell them," she instructed Tabinda.

Tabinda sighed. "Apparently Southfields Athletic has folded. Their coach walked out and nobody was interested in taking over. Some of them are here today looking for a new club."

"They've folded? That's such a shame," I said.

"A shame for us," JJ mumbled. "Who wants them on a team? They're rubbish."

"Erm ... I'd better go back to my dad," Serena said.

"It'll be good to have you on the team if you do decide to join," I told her, not wanting her to think we were all as negative as JJ.

"Thanks."

"I'll come with you," Tabinda told her.

"Yo, Tabs. Before you go, where's Sian? I asked.

"In the middle gazebo, talking to parents."

"Cool."

I tried to link arms with JJ, but she pulled away.

"I'm off home. Got stuff to do."

"Please yourself," I said. I knew if JJ was in one of her moods – and she obviously was – she was best left alone.

"Come on," Petra said. "Time to suck up to the new coach."

"Help, Petra. The word is help."

4

Sian was sitting behind a trestle-table, her long hair falling across her tanned shoulders as she wrote something on her notepad. She was wearing a thin-strapped top rather than a Parrs shirt. Her face was fully made-up: eyeliner, lipstick and everything. Hannah had never worn much make-up to football events and Katie never wore make-up full stop. I took a deep breath, telling myself not to start comparing. I'd promised myself I wouldn't do that. I was "here to help".

I couldn't offer my services immediately. Our new coach was dealing with a group of people: a man with a neck full of tattoos and four girls. I had no problem recognizing one of the girls. It was Crystal, the Southfields captain. She was what my mum would call "a character". On or off the ball,

Crystal would keep up a stream of conversation, not only with her team-mates but also with the opposition, the ref, the stray dog wandering on to the pitch – you named it, she'd talk the hind legs off it. She was doing it now. "An' will you turn up every practice?" she was asking Sian while the others looked on.

"That's the general idea," Sian replied. She glanced up, saw Petra and me and winked.

"And what if we lose? Will you storm off with a cob on?"

"No, no cob ons."

"The last 'un did. She was a right misery guts." Crystal launched into a tirade about her previous coach. Sian tried to stop her but she had no chance. Every attempt was overridden until Sian surrendered and just sat there, nodding. I had to bite my lip to stop myself from bursting out laughing.

"Will they get a game, though, if they join?" The man – I presumed he was Crystal's dad – managed to ask. "Lornton's a fair trek every week and if it's just for 'em to sit on a bench it ain't worth the petrol."

"Everyone gets a chance," Sian told him.

"That's what we've always done," I couldn't help adding.

They all turned then and stared. Crystal looked me up and down. "You're the goalie, aren't you?"

"Yep."

"Thought so. I'd recognize that ginger nut anywhere."

I frowned and was about to tell her I didn't appreciate the ginger thing but forgave her when she continued: "Your lot were the only team that clapped us off at the end of a match without it sounding like you were being sarcastic. That's why we've come 'ere."

"Oh."

"That's nice," Petra told them.

Crystal smiled and revealed a set of shiny new braces. "Anyway, this is Aisha..." She pointed to a girl in a red headscarf and Leicester City top.

"She's a fast runner but her ball control stinks. This is Ebs, short for Ebony..." Crystal continued, indicating a well-built black girl who had a pale orange flower clipped to her hair. "You'll have to stick her in defence. She doesn't move much unless she hears an ice-cream van, then she's off like a champion greyhound."

"Don't lie," Ebony protested.

Crystal ignored her and grabbed the final team member, pulling her by her T-shirt to the front. She was a small, fragile-looking girl with straggly hair and lopsided glasses bound by Sellotape on one side. She was wearing jeans about ten times too big for her and looked as if she wanted to disappear down the nearest hole. "And this is Frances, but everyone calls her Midge," Crystal said. "She's our goalie, but you've no need to worry. She's not half as good as you. Well, not even an eighth, if I'm honest."

I felt embarrassed but Midge just shrugged.

"So what do you reckon? Will we do?" Crystal asked, staring straight at me.

"Sure," I said.

"When's practices start?"

"You'll need to ask Han..." Petra nudged me and I corrected myself just in time. "Sian."

Sian handed her a leaflet. "This Tuesday. If you leave your details, I'll email you."

"Got you," Crystal said and scribbled down hers and everybody else's contact details before leading everyone away with a cheery wave and promises of doughnuts.

When they were out of earshot, Sian shook her head. "Looks like I'll have my hands full there."

"Not half," I replied.

Sian looked at me. "It's Megan, right?"

"How did you know?" I asked, feeling pleased she recognized me. I hadn't spoken to her at the Parrs presentation evening when she'd come to meet everyone. I'd been too busy having my final fill of Hannah and Katie.

"Oh, just a wild guess," she said. "And you must be Petra. Hannah told me you two come as a pair."

Petra offered her hand to shake. "It's nice to meet you, and thank you for taking over as coach. We're really grateful."

"Aw. You're welcome, sweetheart. When Hannah asked me to take her spot, I said of course I would. You've got to bring on the next generation, haven't you?"

"Is there anything we can do to help today?" I asked.

"Not really. I've got everything covered, more or less. Unless my special guest doesn't turn up and then you can go in goal for the penalty shoot-out later."

"Oh, I'd love that," I said. I knew my gloves were in the boot of Dad's car.

"Ah! No need. Here he is now." Sian grinned.

He? The special guest was a he? Joe Hart? Brad Friedel? There was a movement behind me, followed by a voice that chilled me to the bone. I'd heard it often enough, bellowing across the field at the boys' teams while we practised near by. It belonged to

Gary Browne, their ogre of a coach. What was he doing here? "All right, then, flower? How's it going?"

"Really good, thanks, Uncle Gary," Sian said.

Petra and I looked at each other. *Uncle* Gary?

Sian beamed. "Girls, you two are the first to know the good news. Gary's going to be our new assistant coach."

She might have said other things, too, but I didn't catch them if she did because at that moment this huge, dark cloud descended over Lornton. Everyone began rolling round, choking and being sick. People cried out as they doubled over in agony engulfed in thick, poisonous smog. "Help me. Help me please ... arghhh..." Afterwards, Petra told me I'd imagined that bit. She said what actually happened was that I made a gurgling sound and she had to push me out of the gazebo before I could say anything I'd regret. But I'm sure dark clouds were involved. I really am.

5

When I got home I wanted to call Hannah, but Dad wouldn't let me.

"No, Megan, you mustn't," he said, taking the phone out of my hand.

"Dad, it's not like last time," I protested. "This is an emergency."

"No, Megan, it isn't. Trust me on this one. It isn't."

"That's not fair," I fumed. That's the trouble with Dad being a fireman. He always plays the I-know-what-a-real-emergency-is card when I get in a strop.

"Think about Hannah," he soothed. "Think about the position you'll put her in. Sian's her friend."

I wasn't going to give in that easily. "She's not her best friend, though, is she? And I bet she doesn't know about Gary Browne. I bet you anything. She can't stand him. She'll go loopy."

"She can go as loopy as she likes, but it won't make any difference. Who Sian chooses as her assistant isn't any of Hannah's business. She has no say in it."

My bottom lip began to wobble. Dad drew me towards him and gave me a hug. "Come on, Megan. It'll be all right. Browney knows his stuff. His lads have been top of the league for about five seasons in a row."

"That's because they're scared stiff of what will happen if they aren't."

"Don't be silly," Dad said.

I wasn't being silly. I'd seen what Browne was like with his squad. We'd played them for about two minutes once and he'd done nothing but insult them. He'd called them useless and a dozy waste of space. "And he doesn't even like girls," I continued. "He's always saying stuff like, 'Stop playing like a girl', 'Come on, get up; you're not a girl.' You've heard him. You know he does..."

"Well, then, this is a perfect opportunity to show him that playing like a girl is a compliment, isn't it?"

No, I thought, it really isn't.

What can I say about the first practice?

It was dreadful. For a start, there were only nine of us. I'd been expecting at least twenty from the number of people who'd turned up at the open day, but apparently most of them had been locals, enticed over by the smell of doughnuts. A three-year-old won the penalty shoot-out. That tells you all you need to know.

So we stood there, staring at each other. Me, Petra, JJ and Tabinda on one side, Crystal, Ebony, Aisha and Midge on the other, with Serena in-between. The Southfields girls stood out from the rest of us mainly because they were ALL WEARING THEIR SOUTHFIELDS SHIRTS. Way to fit in with your new team, gang! Ebony complemented hers with a matching corsage of pale blue flowers.

I expected Sian to say something about the shirts but she didn't. Nor did Gary Browne, but then he was too far away to see them. He'd perched himself on the bonnet of his car, and just stayed there, his arms folded across his chest like a bored spectator. Fine by me, I thought. The further away the better.

Sian welcomed us all and then made us go round in a circle and introduce ourselves, which was when we found out that Crystal's last name was Ball. "I know," she said, rolling her eyes. "What hilarious parents I've got." When it came to her turn, JJ kept her head bowed and mumbled her name. Midge didn't hear and nudged Crystal, who repeated, "Jenny-Jane Bayliss", at the top of her voice, then added: "The 'ard one."

JJ's head shot up. "What's that supposed to mean?"

"Nothing bad, mush. It's a compliment. You used to scare the pants off us."

"Oh," JJ said, then a smile spread across her face. "Good."

When it was her turn, Serena gave her full name, Serena Helen O'Shea, then, after glancing at her dad, added, "Striker."

"Right, then," Sian said, "let's get warmed up. We'll start with a slow jog round the field."

Petra, me and JJ led the way. We didn't intend to; it's just that we were used to the field and we were used to jogging. Tabinda and Serena weren't far behind, but the Southfields lot were so slow, snails would have lapped them. Ebony was totally puffed out by the time she'd completed the circuit. Hands on her knees, she panted and gasped for breath as if she'd just done the London Marathon. Talk about embarrassing.

We began with the drills. Sian kept them really basic, but you'd think the Southfields four had never seen a ball before. We kicked off with the one where all you have to do is dribble the ball between some poles and then pass it to the next person, who dribbles it back. Simples.

Crystal went first. She managed the first two

poles all right, but then halfway between poles two and three, she attempted what could have been a step-over, but she fluffed it and fell over the ball. She bounced straight back up again and shook her head. "What a muppet," she said, grinning and began again. And did exactly the same thing again: a few metres of fairish dribbling, then the step-over thing followed by a tumble.

Eventually she reached JJ, who dribbled the ball between the poles at lightning speed and delivered it to Aisha. Aisha, like Crystal, began well, then tried the stupid step-over thing with exactly the same result. Petra and I looked at each other. What was going on?

Next up was Tabs, who was less zippy than JJ but just as competent. Crystal tapped me on the shoulder. "Blimey, your girls are quick. Don't expect that from Ebs, will ya? You can have a kip when it's her turn."

I'd like to say she was exaggerating, but she wasn't. Ebony was concentrating so hard on keeping the ball at her feet she barely touched it. The thing moved about a millimetre per tap. While we slid into a coma, Crystal kept up a running commentary. "That's it, gal, nice and steady. You'll get there. Look at that. It's like the ball's glued to yer boot."

That's because it might as well have been.

Serena, as I expected, found the drill straightforward and completed it with ease. Her dad clapped her effort. "Well done, Serena, well done."

Last of all came Midge. I had high hopes for Midge. I don't know why. I thought maybe she'd be like the secret weapon. You know, behind that weedy exterior was talent just waiting to shine.

I was wrong. Midge was useless. Somehow, she managed to take the ball wider and wider between the posts each time, like a toddler scribbling bigger and bigger circles with a crayon. By the time she'd reached the final post she was nearly in the car park. "Calling Midge. Come in, please!" Crystal joked.

I didn't think it was funny. We'd only done one drill and I already knew we were doomed.

It would be pointless to describe the match at the end. It might have been better if we'd mixed, but Southfields wouldn't mix. "We stick together, us," Crystal declared. "Just till we get used to bein' 'ere."

"OK," Sian agreed.

We played four-a-side. It wasn't much fun. Even with a tiny area to play in, I didn't have anything to do in goal. Our side won something like twenty-two–nil. I glanced across at Gary Browne. He was shaking his head as if he couldn't believe what he was seeing. And for once I didn't blame him.

7

"So how did that go?" Eve asked as I waited for Petra at the school gates the next day.

"Don't ask," I said.

"That bad?"

I nodded.

"How many new ones turned up?"

I held up five fingers.

"Is that all? Any of them any good?"

I managed a stiff shake of my head – which was a bit unfair because Serena wasn't bad, but I'd lost the will to speak.

"What about Gary Browne? What was he like? Did he shout?"

Another stiff shake of the head. I opened my mouth to speak, but no words came out. I think

I was coming down with post-traumatic stress. I could have done with a warm blanket and a cup of hot chocolate, to be honest. Eve began to look worried. She put her arm round my shoulder. "It'll be all right, Meggo," she said. "Think about happy things. Remember the cup match where you had your nose broken and there was blood everywhere. Happy things..."

I giggled. Only Eve could have come up with something daft like that as a happy thing. It worked too. By the time Petra arrived, I was talking in full sentences and everything.

I called a Parrs meeting during break. The four of us huddled together in the cloakrooms, moping. "We might as well all wear Southfields shirts," JJ muttered.

"It wouldn't be so bad if there were more players." Tabinda sighed.

"We need Daisy and Dylan back," I said.

Petra shook her head. "They won't come.

They're enjoying ballet too much. I asked."

"It might get better," Tabinda suggested.

"Or it might get worse," JJ said.

The second practice was exactly the same.
Southfields showed up in their Southfields shirts
and murdered every drill Sian did with us. Then
they wouldn't mingle for the match at the end
so got stuffed again. Serena's dad stayed on the
touchlines, clapping every move she made, and
Gary Browne kept his bonnet warm with his bum.

I was in such a fug the following week at school
I forgot to keep an eye on JJ. She'd been on report
for almost two weeks and was due to be signed off
the Tuesday of the third Parrs practice, but she blew
it. She joined in with the rucksack-rugby game, and
in one bad throw managed to turn Alex Almond's
papier mâché model of a volcano into a cowpat.
Her report was extended by another week, taking
her up to the end of the year. That put her in a
fantastic mood for training.

It was all OK until the short match at the end.

"Count me out," JJ said when Tabs handed the bibs round.

"What's wrong? Are you tired?" Sian asked.

"No, I can't be bothered."

"What do you mean?" Sian asked sharply.

"There's no point," JJ said.

"That's a poor attitude. The match is meant to be fun."

"Where's the fun in winning fifty–nil?" JJ asked.

I stepped in to try and stop JJ getting into trouble. "Maybe we could mix up the sides?" I suggested.

But before Sian could respond Crystal shook her head. "No. Not happening. I told you, we don't mind getting beat. We're used to it."

"We're not," I told her.

"You soon will be with us lot." Crystal grinned.

That really annoyed me. I turned to Sian. "Now who's got a poor attitude?"

She frowned at me. "All right, Megan. We're all meant to be on the same side, remember?"

"It doesn't feel like it," I replied. "You haven't even asked them not to wear their old shirts."

Sian's cheeks flushed and Crystal glared at me. "Is there a problem with that, Ginge? Just say if there is."

If she hadn't called me "Ginge", I wouldn't have been so blunt in my reply. "Yes, there is a problem."

"Which is?"

"You lot suck."

"So? You knew that before we even started."

"I didn't think you'd be this bad. You could at least try."

Crystal let out a squeal. "What are you talking about? We've been busting a gut..."

"I wouldn't say 'busting', exactly."

Crystal folded her arms across her chest and began tapping her foot. "No? What would you say, then? Exactly?"

"I have no words to describe it."

"Well, that makes a change."

"Meaning?"

"You never shut up," Crystal said.

I gasped. "Me? Is that supposed to be a joke?"

"Am I laughing?"

"Watch who you're talking to," JJ interrupted.

"Back off, sidekick," Crystal snarled without removing her eyes from mine.

Ebony stepped forward then. "Yeah, back off, sidekick."

"That's enough, ladies," Sian said, making a frantic T-sign with her hands, but everyone ignored her. JJ began arguing with Ebony and Ebony gave back just as good as she got, while Crystal and me eyeballed each other. Petra kept trying to pull me away and the rest of the girls were staring, open-mouthed, until the moment Sian bellowed at the top of her voice, "I said that's enough!"

I jumped, and I know Petra did too. We weren't used to being shouted at. Crystal, however, was. "Oh, here we go," she said, putting her hands on her hips and squaring up to Sian as if she was some kid in the playground. "Another big fat fibber. 'I don't shout,' she says on the open day. Right, that's it. Come on, peeps. Let's go and find my dad."

They stalked off towards the clubhouse. Meanwhile Serena's dad was tugging his daughter's arm. "Come on. I don't want you mixed up in all this. In the car. Now."

"But, Dad..."

"Oh, don't go, Mr O'Shea," Sian pleaded.

"Shambles," he said to her, his face contorted with fury. "An absolute shambles."

8

The four of us stayed to help Sian clear away, but there was a horrible atmosphere. I immediately apologized to Sian, but she didn't respond and continued clearing the cones in silence. I didn't know what to do then. Hannah would have had a quiet word, telling us we'd been out of order but not making a big deal of it. Being blanked was harder to handle. We gathered all the equipment up as quickly as we could.

Not quickly enough to escape Gary Browne, though. He strode up to Sian and gave her a reassuring embrace. "All right, then, flower?" he asked.

"Yes," she said, the wobble in her voice telling him, and us, that she wasn't all right at all.

"Do you mind if I have a few words with your squad?" Gary Browne asked.

"No," she said.

"Right, you four, gather round."

We glanced at each other nervously. Was he going to give us the hairdryer treatment? Screaming in our faces like premiership managers do if their team's played badly?

He didn't do that. When he spoke his voice was quiet and calm. In a way that was worse because it felt like a trick. "Who's this?" he asked, jutting his thumb towards Sian.

"Sian," I replied.

"Nope. Who's this?" he asked again, turning to Tabinda.

"Miss Lewis?" she said, chewing her lip.

He rolled his eyes as if that was the most stupid answer imaginable. "Who's this?" he asked Petra.

"Coach?"

"Finally. Coach. This is your coach. The person who is giving up her spare time, free of charge, to help you. The person who doesn't have to be here with a bunch of ungrateful prima donnas when she could be at home doing a million other things. Next question," he said, addressing JJ. "Who are they?" He pointed to the bottle bank where the Southfields lot were grouped. I blinked. I'd presumed they'd left ages ago. "Who are they?" Browne repeated.

"The Southfields lot," JJ muttered.

He leaned closer. "Don't mumble, lass. I can't hear you," he said and tapped his hearing aid. I hadn't known he used one, but then I'd never been that close to the ogre or his ears before.

"Southfields," JJ muttered but louder this time.

"Wrong," he declared and turned to Petra.

"Ebony, Frances, Crystal and Aisha?"

"Wrong."

Petra frowned. "But..."

It was my turn again.

"Who are they?" His dark eyes burrowed into mine.

I swallowed. I knew the answer he wanted. "Our team-mates."

"Correct. They're your team-mates. Anyone got a problem with that? Yes, of course you have," he continued, not waiting for an answer. "You're the mighty cup-winning Parrs. You don't want to be associated with rubbish like that, do you? Well, I've got news for you." He fished out his BlackBerry and tapped the screen. "Based on my observations over the last two sessions, you..." he said to JJ, "... average. You," he said to Petra, "average. You," he said, pointing to me, "average, and you..." he said, pointing to Tabinda.

"Average?" she ventured.

"Got it in one."

My breathing quickened. We weren't average. We were awesome like Hannah had always told us we were.

Gary Browne didn't wait for a response. He began to steer Sian, who seemed as stunned as we were, towards the bottle bank, adding: "Right. We'll go have words with the other half and you lot can get off home and think about your attitude.

Oh, and bring some mates along next week. Just for Tuesdays, no strings attached. Drag 'em screaming from their Barbie dolls if you have to."

"What sort of mates?" Tabinda called out after him. "Mates who play football or mates who are just mates?"

"Any. And if you can't find any, give us a shout and I'll bring my lads across. They'll sort you."

Average. The word attached itself to me like a flea to a cat, irritating me all week. Every spare moment I had, I searched for volunteers to come along to practice, bribing them with promises of lifts to the ground and snacks once they got there and a free go on the table football in Auntie Mandy's lounge bar afterwards.

Average, I thought as I flung myself at every ball that came my way during the lunchtime matches.

Average. I laughed as I punched in Gemma's number, my heart racing in anticipation at seeing the expression on Gary Browne's face when Gemma made one of her trademark runs at the defence. Average, indeed.

I was gutted when Gemma couldn't come. "I'm not allowed," she apologized. "I've signed a contract with the centre of excellence. I'm only allowed to practise with them. We don't even play in a normal league; we only play other centres of excellence."

"Oh no," I groaned.

Luckily, Lucy and Nika could come, Daisy and Dylan said they'd think about it and Mrs Woolcock thought Holly would be up for it, too. Eve nearly crushed my ribs to pieces when I asked her. "What? I get to be a Parr again? It's a miracle! I'm alive! I'm alive!" she yelled. Eve enrolled two new girls, too. Wendy Li and Cara Stroud, from her after-school club, and Tabinda managed to entice Aleena, who lived near her, with promises of a lift both ways.

The following Tuesday's practice couldn't have been more different. In the end there were loads of us because not only did Daisy and Dylan come along, they brought Ellie Bream, Dylan's second best friend. Serena turned up, too, which I hadn't expected. "She's already signed up here so the

Tigers won't have her back, will they?" I overheard her dad explain to Mr Shah while we all got ready.

A lot of parents stayed to watch, including mine. I think they were all worried after what had happened last week. Mr Shah and my dad had been on the phone to each other several times. They'd agreed that if Gary Browne tried to turn training into a boot camp they'd have to hold an emergency committee meeting.

Maybe Gary Browne had heard because he didn't even have the decency to turn up. He left Sian to deal with everything. I didn't know whether to feel relieved or annoyed, and settled for annoyed. After all the effort I'd made, he could at least have given us five minutes of his precious time.

Sian, on the other hand, with her hair scraped back in a tight ponytail and wearing joggers and a white Airtex T-shirt instead of the tight strappy tops she'd worn in previous weeks, was being super efficient. All the equipment had already been set out and she had a much more confident air about her. I approached her cautiously. We hadn't exactly parted on a high. "Do you need any help, Sian?" I offered as she went round taking everybody's names and collecting in all the permission slips.

"No thank you," she said crisply without even looking at me. "And it's 'coach'."

"She snapped at me," I said to Petra and Tabinda as we jogged round the field to warm up.

"It's not just you. My dad told me that she phoned Crystal's dad and asked him to make sure they didn't wear their Southfields shirts, and I heard her tell Ebony to take her flower out of her hair just now," Tabinda told us.

"She's setting boundaries. You know, like teachers do when they've got a new class," Petra said.

"I hope she doesn't set too many. You know what JJ's like with that," I replied.

Oddly enough, JJ was behaving herself. She'd latched on to the Southfields lot and was acting like some kind of tour guide, escorting them around the field, pointing out various landmarks and pitfalls. "That's where Albert Pikelet lives. You don't wanna kick your ball into his garden, you'll never see it again…"

I knew I should have been doing some befriending too. Crystal and I hadn't spoken to each other so far, apart from a brief nod as we passed. I'd planned to tag on to her group in one of the drills, but I never got the chance.

After we'd warmed up and as Sian was explaining what she wanted us to do in the first drill, I felt a tap on my shoulder. I turned to see Gary Browne and a tall, lanky boy, carrying a net full of balls. Browne beckoned me to follow him. "Over here," he said.

"Why?" I asked as he led me away from the others and over to the far goalpost.

"You're the keeper, aren't you?"

"Yes."

"Better learn how to keep, then, hadn't you?"

"I already know," I said, feeling more ruffled by the second.

Gary Browne laughed out loud. "Hear that, Scotty? She already knows. Ten years old and ready to play for England."

"That's not what I meant."

Gary Browne raised his eyebrows. "That's not what I meant, *coach*."

"That's not what I meant, *coach*."

"Listen, sweetheart," he said. "In a few weeks' time you're going to be playing your first league game. Of the seven members of your team, take a wild guess at who is going to be the busiest on the park?"

I gulped. "Me."

"Correct. Shall we get started, then?"

Scotty dropped the net of balls on the penalty spot and began to untie the string. Gary Browne marched across to the side of the field and began staking out poles at short intervals. I went to the goalmouth, clearing stones away from the line with the tip of my boot, trying to seem composed when I was anything but. Was this some kind of punishment for last week?

For arguing with Crystal and Sian? When I looked up, Scotty had arranged the balls in a long row. My skin prickled. Was he going to blast them at me?

Scotty must have read my mind. "Relax," he said. "They're just lined up so we're not wasting time chasing one ball all the time."

"Oh," I said.

The boy grinned. "I see you're as bolshy as ever. I'll never forget the day you challenged coach to a match against us."

I opened my eyes wide. "You're Scott? The one he kept calling a dozy waste of space?"

"That's me. I'm in the City Academy now."

"Wow."

"He's still a dozy waste of space, though," Gary Browne said, coming to stand alongside Scott. "All right, let's start with the basics. Do you know the 'W' catch?"

I nodded. I'd been doing the "W" catch, where thumbs and fingers make a "W" shape to keep the ball firmly gripped, since day one. Scott threw an easy ball to me and I relaxed. This wasn't a test or a punishment. It was coaching. Proper one-to-one goalkeeping coaching.

After the "W" catch we moved on to different types of throws, then dives and recovery techniques, with Gary Browne giving the instruction and Scott feeding me the balls. It never got boring. The one I liked best was when I had to work my way along the row of poles, diving for one of Scott's shots between the first pair, running to the second pair, then diving another way at the third pair, running to the next and back again. It was to test my speed, footwork and agility. I was so thirsty by the end, I gulped my water down in one go.

"Right, that's enough for one day," Gary Browne said. "Thanks for your help, Scotty. You can get back to your girlfriend now."

"Cheers, coach," Scott said and sauntered off.

I waited for my comment. I'd done OK, I knew I had, but all I got was an instruction to collect the balls and join the others. No "that was excellent" like I'd have got from Hannah or Katie. Not even a "good effort" or a lowly "not bad".

I tried not to feel disappointed. Who needed praise from stupid Gary Browne anyway?

10

After I'd dragged the balls to the storage shed I joined the main group. "You survived, then?" Eve asked.

"Yes," I said. "How about you?"

"It's been immense. Just like back in the day."

I glanced round and could see what she meant. There were loads of new faces, but having the old team sprinkled among them made it feel more normal. Yes, I thought, this was way better than before.

Sian told us all to gather round. "OK, well done, everybody. You've all tried really hard. Time to put what we've learned into practice. Let's have a game, eh? Because there's so many of us we can have seven-a-side."

I instinctively grabbed Eve to be my striker, but

Sian's next instruction put paid to that. "OK, I want you to divide into two groups. Parrs in yellow bibs and non-Parrs – let's call you the All Stars – in blue."

It felt weird seeing Eve, Lucy, Holly and Nika collect blue bibs, but what Sian was doing made sense. Grouping the new Parrs together would get us used to playing as a team. But then came an instruction from Sian that didn't make sense. "I want Midge in goal, Serena and JJ in defence, Crys with Ebz and Megan in the middle and Tabs up front."

"Gotcha," Crystal said cheerily.

"Wardy, you swap in for Tabs in the second half and, Aisha, you swap in for JJ," Sian concluded.

Everyone began to disperse. I thought I'd better double-check Sian's instructions in case I'd misheard. "Excuse me, coach. Are you saying you don't want me in goal?"

Sian nodded. "I feel it's important to be versatile. Experience in outfield positions will do you good."

"OK," I said uncertainly.

"Give Midge your gloves, please."

I don't think I'd ever felt as unhappy in my entire life as when I handed my gloves over to Midge. "They're really sweaty," I told her.

"I don't care. It'll bring me good luck." She grinned.

If letting in five goals in five minutes is good luck, then yes, it did. Holly, in goal at the other end, was less busy. Tabinda had a couple of attempts that went wide but that was it. Not that anyone could blame Tabinda. You need support from your midfielders to score and that wasn't happening. Ebony barely moved and Crystal was the opposite, darting all over the place, then stopping to do her silly attempts at step-overs. Aisha was the best of the four of them but didn't seem to know what to do with the ball when she had it and kicked it anywhere. I wasn't much use, either, if I'm honest. I was still in shock at not being where I belonged.

"Well, that was awesome. Not," I told Petra afterwards.

She frowned. "Didn't you enjoy it? I did."

"I'm not used to playing outfield, I suppose."

"It was interesting, though, wasn't it? Playing as a team for the first time?"

"It depends how you define interesting," I told her.

11

The sessions followed a pattern after that. I was coached by Gary Browne and Scott, then shoved in outfield for the matches.

Occasionally I'd be given five minutes between the sticks but never any longer than that. It began to niggle me after a while. I could see the point of players needing to be flexible and trying out new positions, but why give me one-to-one goalkeeping practice if I wasn't going to use it?

"But you don't need the experience like Midge does, do you?" Petra pointed out when I mentioned it one lunchtime. "Sian's just helping her catch up. Their last coach was only interested in teaching them tricks and ignored the basics. They're starting from scratch, really."

"Oh," I said. That explained the daft step-overs

Crystal did during drills. I frowned. "But if Sian's trying to help Midge catch up, why isn't Midge with Gary Browne instead of me?"

"Dunno. Why don't you ask her?"

"I might."

"On the other hand, that might mean you don't get all that specialist coaching any more and you love it, you know you do."

I scratched my neck. She had a point. I did enjoy it. I'd improved my diving technique and footwork no end, but that just made me keener than ever to try it out in games.

Petra laughed and punched me on the arm. "You know what your problem is? You're never happy. You need to lighten up."

I couldn't, though. Despite giving a hundred per cent during training, I came home feeling more and more despondent. Mum and Dad kept exchanging those "what's wrong with her?" looks and even my cat, Whiskas, stopped hanging out with me. The weather was supportive, though. It decided to match my mood by chucking it down. School was gross. Rain meant "wet play" and being cooped up inside pongy classrooms with steamy windows and flying rucksacks for the last week of term. I was not a happy bunny.

The Year Six Leavers' Service, the day before the end of term, was when I hit rock bottom. The whole school gathered in the hall, even the reception class, who can't sit still for two minutes. Year Six parents and grandparents fanned out round the edges.

I was OK at first. Mr Glasshouse started with a speech about what a credit the Year Sixes had been to Mowborough Primary and wished them all luck at their secondary schools. After that came all the singing and poems about their favourite times and best memories. It was all light-hearted and upbeat, but I couldn't help feeling gloomy. I'd looked up to Mrs Hulley's class, especially Lucy, Eve and Nika. I'd miss them so much.

All too soon it was the final bit. We clapped as, one by one, all the Year Sixes trooped up to receive a dictionary and a book token. Nika, Lucy and Eve were last. As Nika shook Mr Glasshouse's hand, I remembered the tournament we'd been on together last summer at Sherburn Sands. Nika had told us an amazing story about her uncle during the war, her uncle who was here, now, in our school hall, looking so proud and dignified.

Then it was Lucy's turn to shake Mr Glasshouse's hand and I thought of her and Holly, my two defenders, solid as whatever the hardest rock on the planet is. My shoulders were shaking like crazy now. "Are you OK?" I heard Petra whisper.

I nodded, my eyes fixed on Eve. The smartest, the funniest, the coolest, the daftest of all the Year Sixes and all the Parrs. Who was going to replace her? No one because no one could.

"Cheers, dude," Eve said, grinning as Mr Glasshouse handed her the dictionary. "Though I've heard the ending zucks."

It was a rubbish joke, but of course everyone cracked up, which was good because it gave me a chance to hide my face and pretend my eyes were wet from laughing and nothing else.

After that we were dismissed and herded back to our classrooms for the last five minutes of the day. I told Petra I needed the loo and that's where I stayed until I heard the bell go. The second it did, I shot out of the cubicle, grabbed my jacket and dashed across the hall, zigzagging between the groups of grown-ups who were still hanging around after the assembly.

Mum had only just arrived when I reached the gate. "Let's go," I told her before she had a chance to catch her breath.

12

I woke up with awful stomach cramps the next day. After ruling out appendicitis, food poisoning, beriberi and a million other possibilities, Mum sighed. "Are you sure you can't manage to get to school? Just for the last day?" She was due at work soon. Dad had already left.

I shook my head and groaned.

She chewed her lip. "I can't really take any time off. We're short-staffed as it is with the summer-holiday season starting. What if I phone Auntie Mandy?"

I didn't really want to go anywhere, not even Auntie Mandy's, but I didn't want Mum to miss her shift either, so I nodded. Ten minutes later, I was in the car, a hot water bottle pressed to my stomach and a pile of magazines in a tote bag at my feet. "I'll call you at lunchtime to check how you are," Mum promised.

When we arrived at Lornton, Auntie Mandy was at the club door, still in her dressing gown, waiting. "Come on, then, invalid; let's be having you," she said. She put her arm round me and began ushering me indoors. "Leave her with me. I am an award-winning niece-sitter," she told Mum.

In her flat above the club we sat huddled on the sofa, watching the Nickelodeon channel, until about ten o'clock. My stomach cramps had eased off by then and I just felt disconnected from everything, like you do when you are at home and you should be at school. I glanced outside. It was brighter today. They'd be having outdoor break soon. I wondered if Petra was missing me. Probably not, the way I'd been lately.

Auntie Mandy took my restlessness as a sign that I was on the mend. She unwound her arm, leaving my neck feeling cold and bare. "Well, much as I'd like to watch the end of *Hey Arnold!* with you, I'd better get my skates on. Will you be all right?"

"Sure," I said, trying to smile. "I've got TV. I've got biscuits. Everything a girl needs."

"That's the spirit. I'll be in the downstairs bar or the cellar if you need me."

"OK."

Another hour passed and so did the novelty of watching daytime TV. By eleven o'clock my stomach cramps had disappeared and I was mind-numbingly bored. I decided to go downstairs and see if I could help Auntie Mandy.

The main doors were open and a delivery lorry from the brewery was blocking the way. Two burly men were rolling metal casks down a ramp and into the trapdoor leading to the cellar. I could hear Auntie Mandy shouting up from the cellar below and telling them off. "No, I said four bitters and seven lagers."

"We were told it was the other way round."

"Well, you were told wrong."

I decided I'd better leave her to it, so I pushed open the outer door to the main lounge. Auntie Mandy didn't open at lunchtimes, apart from on weekends, so I presumed it would be empty. It wasn't. I could hear talking in the partitioned-off seating area just to my right. "Thanks for coming, everybody," a man was saying. "Sorry for the short notice, but today's the only time we could all make it to go over the agenda. We'll crack on as soon as Tony arrives. He's picking up the minibus from the garage."

Tony? They probably meant Tony Campbell, the secretary of Lornton FC. I had forgotten that officials from the club sometimes had committee meetings here. I was about to scarper when I heard someone ask "Gaz" how it was going with the girls' team. Hmm. This'll be interesting, I thought and pressed my ear to the partition.

"All right, I suppose," Gary Browne replied.

"It's always tough stepping into somebody else's shoes, especially when they were popular," someone said. It sounded like Andy Dixon, the coach of the men's senior team. I knew him quite well. He used to go out with Auntie Mandy.

Gary Browne snorted. "Being popular doesn't mean you're a good coach. All it means is you give the next gaffer a tougher job. Sian had to stop a fight the other week."

My stomach clenched. Another man joined in the conversation now. "A fight? Honestly, girls are as bad as lads these days. In fact, that's what half of them think they are and that's the trouble. They should never have been allowed the vote if you ask me, never mind play football."

Here we go, I thought, expecting them all to agree, but actually the man's sexist comments were derided as "daft" and "ancient". Even by Gary Browne. "You're dead wrong, Jimbo. I've watched a few Women's Super League matches on the telly. They're not bad at all these days. I reckon if you gave women the same opportunities as the men and threw some money at the game they'd be decent."

"Give over," Jimbo scoffed. "You're just winding me up."

"I'm not, not if you start them young enough. The goalie Sian's got is as good as any lad I've ever seen at that age."

I nearly fainted. I thought I was meant to be "average"?

"You mean Megan, Mandy's niece?" Andy asked.

"Yeah, Megan," Browne agreed. "She's a natural. Soaks up everything I tell her."

"Don't tell Mandy. She talks non-stop about her as it is."

"Don't worry, I won't. Telling kids how wonderful they are every two minutes is not my style."

"We've gathered that." Jimbo laughed.

"Well, it's nonsense. I've seen it too often. They're told they're special when they're nothing of the sort and they get above themselves. Start getting all cocky and thinking they're bigger than the team."

"Megan's not like that, though, is she? She always seems level-headed to me," Andy pushed.

"I'm not saying she thinks she's above the team, no, but she does dominate it. The new kids are intimidated by her. That's why I'm giving the lass one-to-one training. It gives the rest of them a chance to bond."

"And is Megan OK with that?" Andy asked.

"Why wouldn't she be? How many Under 11s teams do you know give their keeper individual training? Not many."

There were murmurs of agreement followed by the sound of cups being rattled. "Right. Where's Tony? If he's not here in two minutes I'm off."

My skin prickled. Time to disappear. I turned and scurried back to Auntie Mandy's flat.

13

Auntie Mandy found me staring out of her kitchen window. "Any better?" she asked.

"The tummy ache's gone."

"That's good."

I didn't mention the turbocharged whirlpool that had replaced it. "Auntie Mandy?"

"Yes, m'duck?"

"I think I'd like to go back to school now."

I arrived about ten minutes before the end of lunch. I signed in, gave the secretary my absence note, and headed for the cloakrooms. Petra was trying to slide her reading book into the top of an already jam-packed schoolbag. "Aha! Just the person I need to see," I said and dragged her into the nearest toilet cubicle. We stood opposite each other, our knees touching in the tiny space. "I need to ask you something."

She looked anxious. "What is it? Are you OK? Where've you been?"

"I'm going to ask you some questions and I need you to be honest with me. Promise?"

"Promise."

"Do you think I'm intimidating? You know, at football?"

"No. I don't think so."

"Are you sure?"

"Sure I'm sure."

"Even with the new ones? Crystal and everybody?"

"Crystal wouldn't have squared up to you if she'd been intimidated by you."

I sighed with relief. "That's good."

"They have been a bit..."

"A bit what?"

Petra chewed her lip. "You do want me to be honest, right?"

"Yes. I want you to be totally honest with me."

"OK. They've been a bit wary of you, you know, since the argument."

"Why just me? You, Tabinda and JJ were there too."

"True, but we've made more of an effort to mix since. You haven't, not really."

That's because I haven't had the chance, I thought. I've been on the other side of the pitch, being kept away so I don't contaminate everyone. Except I knew, deep down, that wasn't true. I could have mingled during the warm-ups or the matches or at the end where everyone hung around afterwards. I cringed inside. No wonder they were wary. I'd have been fuming if it had been the other way round. It wasn't like I had a good reason, either. Crystal and co were all friendly enough and they weren't any worse at football than Daisy and Dylan had been at the beginning and they were certainly a lot keener than Amy Minter had ever been.

I let out a low groan. "I've messed up, haven't I?"

Petra squeezed my arm. "No. It's just been a weird start, that's all. Everything will be great when the season begins. Once the newbies hear you make one of your rousing speeches, where you make us feel anything is possible, they'll be flying down the pitch. No one else is like you for those. Only you can do that."

"Really?"

"Really. That's what you do best. You are the bringer-togetherer, after all."

"Bringer-togetherer? That's not even a word. Or two words..."

"It is now. Anyway, I think it's a perfect term for you. That's what makes you such a wicked captain and such a wicked friend."

I should have felt better, but I didn't somehow. I felt too numb. I couldn't let Petra see that, though. There's only so much misery you can dump on your friend before they sink under the weight of it. "Well, thank you, Miss Ward, you've been most helpful," I told her. "And you're not a bad mate yourself, if you don't mind me saying so."

She grinned. "I'm not, am I?"

"Anyway, that's me done. What's new with you? What did I miss this morning?"

"Nothing much. Tidying trays, returning library books and..." Her eyes widened. "Argh. I've got to go. I said I'd help Tabinda with the flowers."

"Flowers?"

"Mrs Marston's leaving present."

"She gets a leaving present? Well, I hope it's a prickly cactus."

When Petra had gone I stared at the floor, thinking about what she'd said. I was thinking about what she'd said while Mrs Marston told me off for being late to registration. I was thinking about what she'd said when she walked into the classroom with Tabinda, her face hidden by the biggest bunch of flowers I'd ever seen. I was still thinking about what Petra had said throughout the afternoon as I helped to strip the wall displays down, ready for the next Year-Five suckers in September. You'll be relieved to know I stopped thinking about what she'd said when I got home. I started thinking about what Gary Browne had said instead. All in all, it was a pretty full-on day, thinking-wise.

By bedtime I'd done that much thinking my head had reached explosion level and Mum and Dad might have been picking blobs of brain tissue from the carpet if Eve hadn't phoned.

"Soooo sorry to call so late, but I didn't see you at school and I'm on holiday tomorrow and I wanted to ask you about the match before I went."

"What match?"

"The England against USA match? At the end of August?"

"Oh, yeah." I'd stuck the flyer on my pinboard, meaning to show it to my parents, but I hadn't got around to it.

"Are you thinking of going? I want to, but my mum's working and Gemma's going with her centre of excellence and Lucy's on a stupid trip to London and nobody else I know is mad about girls' football like you are. So I thought if your mum or dad could take us that would be ace. Only we need to get tickets soon. Please. Pretty please."

"Hang on, I'll ask." I dashed into the front room, grabbed the calendar, double-checked the dates against Mum and Dad's work rosters, double-checked with them it was OK, then returned Eve. "You're on!" I said.

"Yay! What about Petra? Will she come, do you think?"

"I'll ask. I'll ask JJ too and..." I stopped just long enough for one of those light bulbs to appear over my head like they do in cartoons. "Eve?"

"Yup?"

"I'm thinking maybe I'll ask a few more people along, too."

"OK, cool. How many?"

"Maybe eight or nine."

"Baggsy I get the front seat, then. It's going to be squashed in the back."

I laughed and hung up. The bringer-togetherer was back in town.

14

The following Tuesday, I made sure I arrived at practice before everyone else.

"Hello, Megan," Sian said, a puzzled expression on her face when she saw me waiting by the equipment shed. "You're early."

I nodded and reached into my backpack, pulling out a pile of glossy flyers that had come in the post that morning. "I was wondering if we could go to this, coach? It's England Women versus USA at football. The tickets aren't expensive and if we have a party of ten or more we can get them even cheaper. It's at the Keepmoat Stadium in Doncaster. That's about two hours' drive max; I checked on Route Planner. It's worth it to see the top players in the world..." I began running through the names of the US and England players I knew off by heart.

It took a while. "Anyway," I said when I'd finished, "I thought it might be cool if we all went."

"All?" Sian said, one eyebrow raised.

"Yes, all the Parrs. Crystal, Serena, Midge, Aisha, JJ, Petra, Ebony, Tabs and me. Oh, and Eve. It was Eve's idea, so she's kind of essential. And I thought we could ask if we could borrow the Stags' minibus if they're not using it? Then we could all go together and bond and stuff..."

Sian smiled. "I think that would be a great idea, Meggo," she said.

"Me too." I smiled back.

I can never understand people when they talk about the summer holidays dragging. Are they nuts? It seemed to me like one day I was unpacking my bag full of old Year-Five projects and squished-up PE kit and the next I was setting out my freshly sharpened pencils and being blinded by brand-new trainers ready for Year Six. Mind you, there was so much going on in between that I barely stopped to catch my breath. We're talking a week in Cornwall with Mum and Dad and sleepovers at Petra's and me in overdrive at training, trying to prove I wasn't as unapproachable as everyone thought I was. Actually, I didn't need to try that hard. Maybe it was my change in attitude or the warm evenings, but the atmosphere was definitely different.

It helped that Gary Browne and Scott were away for the first fortnight, so I could join in with everyone during the drills. It helped, too, that Ellie, Aleena, Wendy and Cara had decided to join the Parrs properly, because they'd enjoyed the sessions so much. That boosted our squad to thirteen and meant that the seven-a-side matches at the end were way better. Crystal's girls were now comfortable enough around us to split into pairs, rather than demand all four of them played at once, so their dire passing wasn't quite as noticeable. The only glitch was me playing outfield. I hated it. All I wanted was to get back into my goal area, where I belonged. Still, I slapped on a smiley face and said, "Sure, coach," every time Sian directed me into that wide, open space. I'd do whatever it took to prove I was a team player.

Midway through August, Sian arranged a "surprise guest" for one of the sessions. My heart had almost stopped when she mentioned it the week before, thinking it might be Hannah, but it turned out to be Amy Minter. "I asked Amy over especially today because I want her to show you some freestyling moves," Sian explained as Amy stood there, beaming.

"Is this for real?" I asked Petra, confused by the words "Amy" and "freestyle" in the same sentence.

"I guess," Petra replied.

It turned out it was for real. My jaw dropped lower and lower as Amy demonstrated a faultless routine of keepy-uppies and Around the Worlds. "I'll never be able to do nothing like that," Crystal moaned as we all applauded.

"You so can," Amy told her as she blew a strand of hair from her face. "Seriously, if I can, anyone can. I was an absolute klutz at football – ask Megan – until someone taught me these in my spare time. It just takes practice."

"That's the magic word, practice," Sian added.

Amy stayed another half an hour, teaching us how to freestyle, doling out an abundance of gushy compliments such as "Fab", "Lush" and "Way to go". Gary Browne, who'd left early, would have been heaving.

"What do you think?" Amy asked at the end.

"Dead impressive," I told her.

She threw her arms round me and buried her head in my neck. "Oh, Megan. That is just the best thing you could have said. Thank you soooooooooooo much." With a flash of her white teeth and a flick of her hair she was gone.

Eve told me afterwards that Amy had wanted to show her routine at the presentation evening but never got the chance. "But why would she learn how to freestyle? She was never that interested when she played."

"That's the point. She realized she wasn't leaving anything behind. No legacy. She wanted to prove she could do something useful."

"Better late than never I suppose."

I glanced across the field to where Ebony and Aisha were giving Midge and Crystal piggyback rides. A slow smile spread across my face. Football works in mysterious ways.

15

The highlight of my holiday was the England Women v. USA match. It was just the best trip ever. We assembled at Lornton in the afternoon, and while Sian and Gary Browne sorted out the minibus, we swarmed into the loos and covered each other's faces in red and white face paint. The place was such a mess by the time we'd finished. "Sorry, Auntie Mandy," I told her as we streamed out again.

"Yeah, sorry, Auntie Mandy," Crystal chipped in, swinging her replica flag around her like a cape.

On the minibus we sang "Here We Go" and "Three Lions on Her Shirt" all the way to the stadium while scoffing about fifteen buckets of pick 'n' mix between us. No wonder we were as high as kites by the time we reached Doncaster.

We weren't the only ones enjoying ourselves. Hundreds of girls' teams from all over England seemed to be descending on the Keepmoat, all wearing their team kits or England shirts. There were loads of boys, too, and families, not to mention TV cameras. Eve and I scoured the crowds for Gemma, but we couldn't see her. "I think she's in a different stand from us," Eve grumbled.

I bought two programmes, one for me and one for Mum and Dad. Now that Cara, Wendy and Ellie had joined the Parrs there hadn't been enough room for parents on the minibus, although Mr Shah had wangled a place somehow. I clasped the glossy programmes to my chest, knowing I'd keep them for ever.

Upstairs, the red and white Doncaster Rovers stands were filling fast. People were chanting and waving scarves or huge sponge hands. Over on the far side from us, someone started banging drums while behind me a group began blowing vuvuzelas. A giant flag appeared out of nowhere and was passed above our heads like a billowing nylon cloud. We all had to reach out and make sure it kept moving all around the stadium.

Meanwhile, down on the pitch, cheerleaders danced to "We Will Rock You" and everyone joined in, swaying and singing along. I leaned forward and tapped Aisha on the arm. "How brilliant is this out of ten?" I asked her.

"Eleven." She grinned back.

"They're coming out! They're coming out!" Eve squealed.

Everyone rose and cheered their head off as the two teams emerged from the tunnel, England in all-white, the States in black with cerise piping. I could feel my chest bursting with pride. Here they were. The best women footballers of their time, of my time. It was overwhelming. Unreal, almost. Seeing my heroes lining up for the national anthems. Kelly Smith and Rachel Unitt. Rachel Yankey and Jess Clarke. Jill Scott and Fara Williams. Casey Stoney and Faye White. Alex Scott and Karen Carney. Natasha

Dowie and Stephanie Houghton. And best of all, in their separate purple tops, Rachel Brown and Karen Bardsley, the two keepers. (Brown was starting. Bardsley was on the bench.) I stared at them in awe. One day, I thought. One day that could be me.

My eyes then travelled along the line of the USA players, resting longest on Hope Solo. Hope Solo, winner of the Golden Glove for best goalkeeper in the last FIFA World Cup. Hope Solo. Ranked number 1 in the world. It was too much to take in.

Then all the players shook hands, swapped pennants and took up their places. The ref blew her whistle and it was game on.

At the beginning, the USA's passing and distribution was better, but it was Yankey who scored first with a stunning volley after twenty minutes. The USA replied immediately with a header from Amy Rodriguez and they made it one–two at the break when Sydney Leroux got a lucky deflection off Rachel Unitt.

"Goals just on half-time are killers," I groaned.

The second half was dizzying end-to-end stuff with both sides creating loads of chances. It stayed at one–two until the last minute of injury time when Dowie was brought down in the box. Penalty! Yes! Smith took it and buried it in the bottom left-hand corner of the net after Solo guessed wrong for once and dived the opposite way. Two–all, the score at full-time.

After the whistle blew and everyone had clapped the teams off the pitch, I didn't want to move. I just sat there in a trance as the rows began emptying all around me. Petra had to pull me away. "Come on or you'll end up in lost property," she joked.

There was a massive queue for the ladies on the way out. Sian made half of us wait by the bar area with Gary Browne and Mr Shah while she took the other half in with her. It was then that I spotted Gemma walking in the opposite direction. I pointed her out and we all yelled, but there were too many people between us and she didn't hear. "Don't they look smart?" Eve said as the squad, all in navy blue tracksuits with "City Girls' Academy Centre of Excellence" written on their tops, filed down the exit.

A lump came to my throat. "Very smart," I said.

I don't know why I did what I did next, but when Sian took the second cohort into the loos, I went to stand next to Gary Browne. He was deep in conversation with Mr Shah, so I waited until they noticed me.

Tabinda's dad acknowledged me first. "Hey, Meggo. Did you enjoy yourself?"

"It was brilliant," I said. "I thought they both played really good attacking football."

"We were just saying we weren't sure if that should have been a penalty."

"Course it should," I said. "It was a deliberate foul. She took her feet right from under her."

Mr Shah laughed and patted me on my head. "That's what I love about you, Meg; your passion. Oh..." He stopped and pulled out his mobile. "S'cuse me while I take this."

The second Mr Shah turned away, I asked the question that was burning inside me. "Coach, do you think I could get into a centre of excellence?"

"Not this year, no. You need a bit more experience at grassroots level. Besides, the trials have already been."

I bit back my disappointment. "What about next year?"

"Next year?" He looked me up and down, scratched his nose, breathed sharply in and out, then nodded. "Next year. Without a shadow of a doubt."

A shiver ran through me. "Thank you," I said and walked off.

16

Sian phoned me the next morning.
"Hey! Have you recovered from all that
excitement yet?"

"Almost."

"Thank you so much for arranging the trip to
the Keepmoat. I've already had parents calling
to say how much their daughters enjoyed it.
Well done, you."

"It was Eve's suggestion really and you did all
the work, driving the minibus and stuff."

She groaned. "Don't mention the minibus. It still
reeks and I've had the windows open all night."

"Oops."

I'd forgotten that Crystal and Ebony had puked
up in the back after too many sweets and hot
dogs.

"Anyway, I wanted to run a couple of changes by you, if that's OK?" Sian said.

"Sure."

"First is that Gary's team practices have been rescheduled so they clash with ours. He's going to be around if I need any help, but he won't be able to give you the one-to-one coaching any more."

"No worries. Will you be all right on your own?"

"I should be. I think I'm getting the hang of it now."

"Definitely."

"Anyway, Katie's back in October. The backpacking thing's not working out like she thought it would..."

I gasped. "Katie's coming back? That's wicked."

"Thought you'd be happy. And while you let that sink in, the next thing I wanted to talk to you about is choosing the new captain."

I held my breath, praying she wasn't going to say what I thought she was going to say. "OK."

"What I was thinking was..."

She paused, making things worse.

"... What I was thinking was that whoever wins player of the match one game is captain the week after, on a rotation system."

"That's brilliant," I told her and let out the biggest sigh of relief ever.

"Really?"

"Really."

"You don't mind? I know you were the captain under Hannah, but I think this is a fairer way. Everyone gets a go then."

"Sure. Whatever you think is best."

"Oh, you are such a sweetheart. I thought you might be upset."

"No, not at all. I'm glad. Who'll be the first one? I think you should choose Serena. It'll keep her dad off your back for one match at least. Or Petra. She's quiet but sensible."

"Good thinking, although I was going to ask you, as a reward for all your hard work."

"That's really mint of you, but I can't. I won't be there."

"Oh. How come?"

I swallowed, hardly able to believe what I was going to say next. "You know how you're always saying players need to be flexible and try new things?"

"Yes."

"Well, I've decided to be flexible and try new things. I'm leaving the Parrs."

Final Whistle

Bit of a dramatic ending, huh?
Looking back, I can't believe I did
that, leave so abruptly. That's the
thing about being a goalie. You have
to make quick decisions.

I blame Gemma Hurst. If she hadn't
walked by at the Keepmoat looking
so ... Eve said smart, but it was
more than that. It was more an aura
she gave off, like, here I am. This
is where I was destined to be, with
this centre of excellence. I knew at
that moment I wanted that to be my
destiny, too, if I was good enough to
get in. When Gary Browne said I was,
that did it.

Of course, me being me, my
imagination didn't stop there. By the
time I'd brushed my teeth that night
I'd not only been accepted into the
centre of excellence, I was already

at one of the elite camps where they train future England players and I'd been tipped for the Under 15s as the youngest keeper ever. Yeah, yeah, I know. Dream on. But what's wrong with aiming high? That's what sportswomen do.

The trouble was, just because Browney said I could get into a centre of excellence didn't mean it was a done deal. Hundreds of girls compete for only a handful of places and there are even fewer spaces for goalkeepers. I needed to set myself tough challenges leading up to the trials, and what could be a tougher challenge than leaving the Parrs?

I know it sounds drastic. Why leave when everything was going so well? When your best mate's on the team and your auntie runs the

clubhouse? When you've warmed to the
new coach, found out your old one's
coming back and you like everyone
on the squad? Well, that's the whole
point. It was too easy. The last
thing I needed when I was coming up
for trials was a season of feeling
comfortable.

I hope all this doesn't sound
like I was deserting the team. If
I'd thought for one second that the
Parrs would collapse without me I
would have stayed, but I knew they'd
be absolutely fine. Sian was growing
as a coach and her team were growing
around her. Petra, Tabinda and JJ were
coming into their own. It was their
turn to shine. They didn't need me.

A week after the trip to the
Keepmoat, the new term started. Mrs
Hulley greeted us all with a massive

smile and a spelling test. I liked
her instantly. Year Six was going
to be OK. In other news, the twins,
now in Year Five, informed us that
they'd given up ballet and were
trying out judo.

Meanwhile, across the other side
of town, Mowborough High School had
a new girls' football team. Founding
members? Eve Akboh, Nika Kozak, Lucy
Skidmore and Holly Woolcock, of
course. I haven't heard how Gemma and
Amy are getting on at St Agatha's,
but I hope I'll see them at the big
reunion planned for October when
Katie comes back.

As for me, well, I am proud
to announce I am the new keeper
for Mowborough Primary School. Mr
Glasshouse was really chuffed when

I told him I'd unexpectedly come on to the transfer market. "That's splendid news. Nice to have you aboard, Fawcett," he said.

It was nice to be aboard, too. Nice and scary.

Anyway, that's it. That's my story, from beginning to end.

I hope you've enjoyed it.

And remember, if you want to play football, all you need to start with is a playing field and one mate. It helps if an awesome person called Hannah happens to jog by and stops to give you some coaching tips, but if not, you can always check out your nearest team on the FA website.

Love and penalty saves,
Megan F xxx